CHILLS
IN THE
NIGHT

Tales That Will Haunt You

WHEN ALL THE BOYS in the school join in Brian's game of statues, no one can quite explain how he freezes them in such strange positions; it's as if "ice crystals had formed all through them"— they couldn't move even if they wanted to . . .

In this and seven other chilling stories, Jackie Vivelo adds a subtle twist to traditional ghost stories as she explores deeper and darker secrets and emotions. Who or what is behind the ghostly lights in the schoolhouse? How could Molly's ruby and diamond necklace possibly disappear if no one left the room? What strange creature is Harry's dog Ransom pursuing in his dreams? And why can't Nathan find the story in his ghost book that he read only days before?

Jackie Vivelo is fascinated by mysteries, by questions that do not have everyday answers. As in her first collection of ghost stories for DK, *Chills Run Down My Spine*, each of the stories in this book explores a different dimension of human mystery. Certain to haunt the memory, these stories are ideal for sharing by reading aloud.

Jackie Vivelo

CHILLS
IN THE
NIGHT

Tales That Will Haunt You

A DK Ink Book

The author wishes to thank her nephew Christopher Lamirata,
whose house she borrowed together with its disappearing floor.

The following stories originally appeared in *A Trick of the Light* (G. P. Putnam's Sons, 1987): "A Dog Named Ransom," "A Plague of Crowders," "A Game of Statues," and "The Fireside Book of Ghost Stories." "Ghost of Christmas Past" originally appeared under the title "Appalachian Blackmail" in *Alfred Hitchcock Mystery Magazine*, January 1994.

First American Edition, 1997

2 4 6 8 10 9 7 5 3 1

Published in the United States by
DK Ink, an imprint of DK Publishing, Inc.
95 Madison Avenue, New York, New York 10016

Visit us on the World Wide Web at http://www.dk.com

Published in Great Britain by Dorling Kindersley Limited.

A catalog record is available
from the Library of Congress.

ISBN 0-7894-2463-0

Color reproduction by DOT Gradations Ltd.
Printed and bound in Great Britain
by The Bath Press.

Jacket illustration by Jennifer Eachus

CONTENTS

When
Nothing's
There
At All

THE RAIN STARTED ON MONDAY, a drizzle from a gray sky. On Tuesday, the drizzle turned to a downpour.

It rained all day. All through the night, rain pounded on rooftops. On Wednesday, the school bus felt as wet inside as out. Wet children in wet clothes slid across wet seats. Drops of rain beaded on the windows.

Children ran through the rain into the school, dripping water across the floor.

"Rainy days bring out the worst behavior," Mrs. Adams, the reading teacher, said, as the dark morning wore on. She separated the class into small groups to read aloud.

"May we tell stories?" Lindy asked for her group. Steven, Gerry, Lucy, Lindy, and Barbara had the corner of the room farthest from the door. They were sitting in a circle on a rug below windows that reached to the ceiling.

Mrs. Adams hesitated, looked at the rain falling

beyond the windows, and said, "Yes, you may."

Outside the classroom, water slid down the windows. The sky was almost black. The rain shut out all the rest of the world. The students in Lindy's story group felt a little like they were on a ship at sea with nothing around them but water for miles and miles. Steven was careful to pull his legs onto the rug with the rest of the group, instead of sprawling half off it the way he usually would.

"Just don't tell ghost stories," begged Lucy.

"Yes! Let's do ghost stories," Barbara said. "It's as good as nighttime."

Gerry said, "Lindy, you start. It was your idea to ask if we could tell stories."

Without waiting for another protest from Lucy, Lindy began, "Once in the dark of night a man left his room in an old hotel and counted the steps as he went down the stairs. '. . . fourteen, fifteen, sixteen,' he counted as he reached the bottom. Later, when he started back up in the pitch darkness, he counted the steps again.

"Finally, he reached fifteen and then sixteen. He was sure he was back at the top of the stairs right in front of his door. But no, there was one more step. 'Seventeen,' he counted. Then, 'Eighteen, nineteen, twenty.' "

"That's creepy. How could there be more stairs?" Lucy asked.

No one had an answer.

"I know another story," Steven said. "It's really short."

Lucy wrapped her arms around her knees and pretended not to care.

"It was the middle of the night, and a man was all alone in the cemetery," Steven said. "Just then he heard a cough behind him."

"What happened?" Lucy asked, because she had been listening even though she pretended not to.

"That's it. That's the whole story."

"No one was there. No one at all. But someone coughed?" Barbara asked.

"That gives me the creeps," Lindy said.

"That story's not so scary," Gerry said. "I can think of something worse than that."

"What can be worse than when something's where nothing should be?" Lindy asked.

"Is it a story?" Lucy asked.

"Sort of. Only it really happened. It didn't happen to me. It happened to my cousin. I don't think I could stand it if it happened to me."

"So tell us," Steven insisted.

"Are you sure you want to hear it?"

Everyone nodded, even Lucy.

"A couple of years ago, my cousin—he's fourteen now—told me this story about something that happened to him when he was a lot younger."

Lindy, Barbara, Steven, and Lucy sat quietly. Lucy chewed a button on her sweater, but no one made a sound. Everyone in the group wanted to know what can be scarier than something that's *there* when nothing should be. They waited and listened as

Gerry told his story:

Dan was four years old when his family moved from an apartment in the city to a large, old house in the country. The house was big for four people, and it needed a lot of work. The way Dan described it, the house had a monster of a furnace in the basement, as well as rats. He was scared to go down there. In the attic, a colony of bats rose up in a cloud whenever anyone opened the door. So, he didn't go into the attic either. Dan's dog didn't like it any better than he did. His older brother Billy always shrugged and said, "It's a house in the country. What do you expect?"

In between the attic and basement was the big house that had once been a funeral parlor.

Dan was afraid of his house from top to bottom, and who can blame him?

Besides staying out of the attic, Dan had other things he did to protect himself. For instance, at night he would reach over the side of his bed to touch the floor, just to be sure it was still there. Sometimes he imagined he was lying in bed with nothing at all around him. Touching the floor let him know that everything was still where it should be. Maybe not being scared just means you don't have any imagination.

Anyway, one night when Dan was nearly eight, he woke up and it was completely dark. He imagined, as he sometimes did, that the floor had disappeared. He rolled onto his side and reached as far as he could until his fingers touched the polished wood of his bedroom floor. On most nights, he would feel reassured, wrap his arms around his teddy bear Tink, and fall asleep again, but this time the house felt wrong.

Everything was completely quiet, and the very quietness seemed thick and heavy. Dan thought he could almost hear the silence. He couldn't hear his older brother breathing in the twin bed on the other side of the room. He didn't hear any of the ordinary creaks and snaps of the old house. He didn't hear the rustlings of bats or other creatures. He couldn't hear the rattling of the pipes that meant the old furnace was working. He couldn't hear the wind. He couldn't hear his father or mother. He couldn't hear anything at all.

First, he whispered, "Billy?"

But Billy didn't answer.

He tried again louder this time, but still nothing. He listened to the silence in the room and knew his brother wasn't there.

"Mom!" Dan called, softly at first and then louder. No one came.

"Dad!" he called, and still nothing happened.

Beginning to feel really scared now, Dan called his dog, Gunner. Gunner didn't come either.

Dan sat up and looked at Billy's bed. It was empty. He didn't want to get up and cross the dark room into the silent hallway. He lay in bed and tried to go back to sleep, but he found himself listening for Billy to come back to bed. After what seemed like hours, he sat up on the side of his bed, found his slippers and put them on, then stood up, hanging onto his bear Tink with one hand. He thought he would just go to the door and call again for his parents.

At the door of his room the silence seemed thicker than ever. Dan shook his head and stepped out into the hall.

No matter what happened, he intended to see his parents. At the door to his parents' room, he paused and called out.

No one answered.

The house seemed even quieter here.

Dan edged his way over to the big bed, sliding one foot after the other. He still hadn't given up the idea that the floor might not be there when you couldn't see it.

When he reached the bed, he called out again. No one answered. He touched the bed and it was cold. He felt the bed and no one was there.

Dan had been scared before; now he was panic-stricken. He hurried from the room to the bathroom at the end of the hall, thinking Billy might be there.

The bathroom was empty.

The absolute quiet in the house had been telling him it was empty. But now Dan *knew* that he was all alone in the house, that house with bats in the attic, rats in the basement, and a one-time funeral parlor in between.

He found the stairs. Clinging to the stair rail with one hand and still holding his bear Tink in the other, he made his way down. In the front hall, he turned on the lights. Then he went from room to room turning on the lights. The living room, the dining room, the bathroom, the kitchen, the pantry, his father's office— all were empty.

"Dad!" Dan called. "Dad? Where are you?"

Dan stared at the door to the basement, but he couldn't bring himself to open it. He went to the back door and turned on the outside light. He stared out for a long time, but he didn't see anyone. Softly, he called, "Mom? Dad?"

When he couldn't stand the silence any longer, he opened the door and called for Gunner again. Maybe the dog was outside, he thought. But Gunner didn't come. How could everyone be gone? Somebody should be there.

Finally, he turned back and looked at the dreaded door to the basement once more.

He had to open it. He was going to find other people no matter what.

He turned the doorknob and eased the door open slowly. For a while he stood well back in the kitchen and called, "Billy, are you down there? Mom? Dad? Is anybody down there?"

He started to get hoarse, so he fell silent. Still, he didn't want to look into the basement.

Maybe something had gone wrong with the furnace; maybe everyone was working on it.

Dan looked through the door and saw that the light wasn't on in the basement. He switched it on and waited for the scurrying noises to stop before he stepped onto the stairs. Halfway down the stairs, the monster came into view.

Dan swallowed hard and stared at the ugly old furnace. Living with it hadn't changed his opinion. It was huge, orange and gray, with two big arms—one that turned up and one that turned down. It also made gurgling, chewing sounds. There was no way Dan was going down there. He spun around and got up the stairs as fast as he could, still carrying Tink.

He went back up the main staircase, ran down the hallway past the empty bedrooms, and found the door to the attic stairs. He only hesitated a moment before he opened it and climbed up. He stood with his head just above the floor and looked around the attic. Dan could see the slatted vent at the end of the room that was the bats' entranceway to the attic they used as their cave. Overhead he saw the rafters of the house; he looked at the floor and saw it was littered with bat droppings. No one ever came up here. No one was here now.

Dan stood frozen to the step.

Just then something small and black flew at his head.

Quickly Dan ducked to miss the swooping bat and nearly slipped on the narrow step. He caught the rail and climbed down, stumbling as he went.

At the foot of the steps, Dan closed the door to the attic. He felt numb.

Still holding onto Tink, he went back to the main stairs and sat down on the top step. He would wait until someone came home. He wrapped both arms around Tink and held the bear close to him.

He sat there, listening to the silence. Resting his head against his bear, he waited. Sometimes he lifted his head and looked around hopefully. Sometimes he cocked his head and listened harder. All the while he hugged Tink. Out of everything he trusted in the world—his parents, his brother, his dog—only a stuffed bear remained. Sometimes Dan whispered to Tink.

All around him the quiet old house waited. Dan remembered that it had been a funeral parlor, and he thought of dead bodies in coffins. He tried not to, but he even imagined candles burning. Suddenly he smelled flowers.

He didn't see or hear anything. Then, slowly, he began to grow cold. The cold seemed to come up through the floor. It chilled his hands and his feet. Dan stopped whispering to Tink and just listened. He felt cold all the way through. Blackness and silence and cold moved up through the house. It came from below him, maybe up from the basement, rising like evening damp or nighttime chill. A cold, dark cloud of silence moved up the stairs toward him.

The cold was a real thing. So was the silence. So was the blackness. All of them were nearby. Dan felt them moving toward him. The smell of flowers made him choke. Soon the cloud would cover him too. Dan had trouble breathing. Something dreadful was creeping up the stairs one step at a time, nearer and nearer. For a moment he was frozen and couldn't move at all.

He grabbed the stair rail beside him and pulled himself slowly up, in a struggle that was a little like swimming in pudding. He was holding the rail in one hand and Tink in the other when he felt something grab Tink and tug.

Then Dan screamed. He yelled as loud as he could. He called out for his mother, his father, his brother, his dog. He could feel Tink slipping out of his grasp.

Suddenly Tink was pulled away, and Dan ran. He reached his room and slammed his door with the cloud of dark silence moving up behind him.

"Billy!" he called. "Billy!"

No answer came from the bed on the other side of the room. Dan knew there was still no one there.

He grabbed the extra blanket from beside his bed, piled up all the bedclothes he could find, and climbed under the covers where he lay shaking and shivering.

His teeth were chattering. He knew he'd hide in his bed, awake and terrified, for the rest of the night.

Would morning come?

Would he find anyone if it did?

Maybe he was all alone in the world with that silent, cold blackness waiting outside for him.

The next thing he knew, sunlight was streaming through the window.

Dan sat up in bed and saw his brother sitting on the bed on the other side of the room, putting on his shoes.

"Where were you last night?" Dan asked.

"What do you mean?"

"I woke up in the night and you weren't here."

"Of course, I was there! Where else would I be?"

"You weren't in your bed. I called you, and you didn't answer."

"You were dreaming!" Billy said.

"I looked at your bed, and it was empty," Dan insisted. "You weren't there."

"Give it a rest!" Billy said. "You had a dream."

Dan got dressed and went downstairs for breakfast. His mother and father were both in the kitchen. Dan asked for oatmeal and his mother gave him a bowl of oatmeal with sugar and berries. He ate quietly, feeling dull and still half-asleep.

As he ate, he thought about the night before. It hadn't felt like a dream, but how could it be real? Was Billy right?

"Don't fall asleep in your oatmeal!" Billy said, nudging him.

Their dad walked over and opened the door to the basement. In a moment he came back.

"That one, too," he told their mother.

"I don't understand it," she said. "Every light on this floor of the house! We could forget one, but you know we didn't leave every light on!"

All the lights on?

Dan lifted his head, wide awake now. Only Dan knew who had turned on the lights. Now fully alert, Dan noticed that his bear Tink wasn't by his side.

"Where is Tink?" Dan asked, as his parents stood

staring at each other beside the basement door. "Have you seen Tink?"

"Probably still in your bed," Billy told Dan.

But Tink wasn't in the bed. Tink wasn't upstairs or downstairs. Dan and his mother and father and his brother Billy searched everywhere, but that bear never showed up again.

"That old teddy bear named Tink," Gerry said, "the one Dan'd had since he was a baby, disappeared that night. Dan and his family looked for it, but no one ever saw it again."

Right after reading class, the students went to lunch. The room was noisier than usual, but some of Mrs. Adams's students were glad for the noise. Not one of them wanted to hear silence. They tried not to look at the dark, rain-streaked windows or think about the blackness outside. How could they be sure the world was still there?

The
Haunted
Schoolhouse

THE SMELL OF YEAST-RISEN BREAD is enough to make you think you are hungry when you're not. When you're as hungry as I was that afternoon, it was enough to make me beg.

My sister Molly saw the look on my face and spared me the humiliation.

"Betsy, you can have one buttered roll, provided you don't tell anyone else. If I have everybody in here asking for bread after school, we won't have any left for supper."

She had a point. With seven children still living at home, we fed a crowd at every meal.

"So how did you get home early enough to bake the rolls?" I asked, licking a drop of butter from the corner of my mouth.

"My math teacher went on a trip with the band, so we just had a study hall for the last period."

"And you skipped it."

She shrugged. "They'll never know. No one ever

notices anything in that school."

"Well, somebody's noticed a ghost in the school," I told her.

Hearing the noise of a scuffle in the hallway, I hurriedly wiped my mouth and chin to get rid of telltale crumbs.

"I smell br-r-read," my little brother James said, drawing the word out like an incantation.

"What about a ghost?" my older brother Joe asked.

"Here, Betsy," Molly said, covering the rolls to save them for supper, "you peel the potatoes while you tell us all about the ghost. We're going to surprise Mama with supper."

"Yeah, Betsy, what's going on?" my brother Cliff asked. Cliff was one year younger than I was, but that was sometimes hard to remember because he was—I don't want to say "smarter." It's just that Cliff was born knowing more than most people ever learn.

"There's not much to tell," I said. "People have been seeing lights in the school when no one's there."

"I heard about it, too," James told them. "There've been funny noises, like chains clanking."

"Nobody in eighth grade has said anything about it, so how come the third and fifth graders are talking about it?" Joe asked. "I think this is a joke somebody's playing on you little kids."

I didn't like being called one of the "little kids" any more than James did. I got busy gouging the eyes out of the potatoes. Joe could hear about the school's ghost when someone else decided to tell him. I wasn't going to tell him anything more.

At school the next day, Mrs. Winslow said, "Betsy and Billy Ray, would you two go get some crepe paper from the storeroom by the auditorium?"

I'd rather have had my teeth pulled than do anything with Billy Ray Bobble, but Mrs. Winslow's word was law in fifth grade. Before we left the classroom, she told us to bring back one package of orange and one package of black paper to make Halloween decorations for our classroom.

As soon as the door closed behind us, Billy Ray clumped off down the hall. When I reached the storeroom, I found him standing in the middle staring around.

"It ain't here."

"What?"

"I told you plain. The box ain't here. You go tell her we can't find it."

"I will not!" I said indignantly. "I'm going to look."

"I already looked."

"Then we'll look somewhere else. Maybe somebody put it in the wrong room."

We began to check the closets around the auditorium, four of them altogether, but had no luck.

"What about upstairs?" Billy Ray suggested, nodding toward the spiral steps that rose at one side of the backstage area.

We clattered up the metal steps and opened the door of the small storeroom above the stage.

What we saw shocked us both into silence.

The room was empty except for a pile of old cushions covered with a rumpled sheet and a filthy blanket. We were looking at someone's bed.

Billy Ray was first to break the silence.

"So it ain't no ghost. Wait'll they hear."

He went clanging down the steps as I tried to talk to him. I wasn't sure we should tell everybody.

Billy Ray didn't listen to me. By the end of the day, everybody knew someone had been sleeping at the schoolhouse. Our small coal-mining town only had one schoolhouse.

"Who'd want to sleep in the school?" my brother Joe asked that afternoon.

Privately, I asked Cliff the same question.

"Only somebody who didn't have anywhere else to stay, I guess."

For the next week we were checked in and out of school each day. A tally was kept to see that no one stayed behind. When the principal was sure that no one, not even the janitor, was still in the building, he personally checked the locks on all the windows, locked the doors, and then added padlocked chains. Reports of ghostly lights still continued. The principal, however, insisted that no one could get into the building.

"Ghost? Hah!" Joe taunted me. "I told you there wasn't any ghost."

We were walking home from school late in October. Leaves were turning and a chill was in the air.

"So, who do you think was in the school? And why are people still seeing lights at night?"

"Probably it was some escaped lunatic," Joe said. "The lights people think they're seeing now are just reflections."

The mystery of the ghost was solved as far as my brother was concerned. All we had really done, though, was change the puzzle of the lights in the school at night for the puzzle of who had been using the bed in the storeroom above the stage.

The next day ghosts and mysteries were lost from our lives, wiped out by the nightmare of every coal-mining town. Around midday a section of the mine caved in. Before one o'clock someone brought word to the school and the news spread to every classroom.

School went on, but everyone knew we were just marking time. The teachers, the students, the big kids, the little ones—all were waiting. We didn't know how many men were missing. Someone told me twelve men; someone else said only three. But no one knew for sure; maybe no one had been trapped. Then again, maybe Papa was trapped. That was how everybody thought when we heard "cave-in." How many? Who? Could one of them be ours? Some of the questions on that long afternoon made my throat close in pain. Before long my nose was running. Nobody noticed. Half the class was sniffling.

As soon as we were dismissed, we each raced for

home, in a ragtag line, arriving quickly and separately. Home, of course, was where word would be.

"Who?"

"What?"

The questions were the same and simple. One by one we learned the facts as Mama knew them.

At least four men were missing. And, yes, Papa was one of them. Mama was calm and dry-eyed as she told us. Cindy and Tommy, who were too young for school, were clinging to her, sensing something was wrong no matter how normal Mama sounded.

"Where were they?" Joe asked. "I'm going over there."

"No, you aren't," Mama said, steel in her voice. "You'll stay here with me. They have a crew trying to clear the entrance. The men were in the old Arcturus spur."

"I want to be with the rescue crew," Joe insisted.

"Joe," Mama said quietly, "they don't know how bad the cave-in is. It may be just the entrance. It may be the whole tunnel."

On that last sentence, Mama choked and turned her head away. Joe took off out the door, as James and Cliff stared after him.

"Come on," my sister Molly said. "We'll get supper."

While we were working in the kitchen, my oldest sister Amanda came home. She had gotten married just the summer before.

"I came as soon as I heard," she said, sitting down to talk to Mama while the rest of us went on with the daily routine.

I had been eight when the last disaster struck the mine. I knew that last cave-in had to be on everybody's mind. The landslide had closed an entire spur. A crew of six men had been lost, with no bodies ever recovered. The sealed shaft became a tomb for the lost men.

I knew Jamie Dawson, whose father had been one of the men in that crew. Jamie was too much older than I was to be a friend, but in our town everyone knew everyone else. Several times when I was out walking, I had come across Jamie. At first I only noticed that, like me, he spent a lot of time walking in the hills. Then over the course of a year, I learned that the only place he walked was the area of the collapsed mine shaft. I was always careful to leave him alone, respecting his privacy. A couple of times I spotted him lying on the ground. Then one day I found him kneeling with his head to the ground. That time I walked right up to him.

He sat up, embarrassed to be caught, even by a kid years younger than he was.

"I—I was listening for footsteps. You know, like an Iroquois scout."

"Then you didn't do a good job," I told him. "I walked right up to you before you noticed me."

"Yeah, maybe it doesn't work so well."

"Maybe you weren't listening for what was on the surface."

He looked at me sideways, considering, and then his

shoulders dropped.

"You're a snoopy kid, you know that."

I didn't mind what he said. I could see he wasn't mad, just really tired, and I figured he needed to tell someone. I stood my ground and didn't say anything. In a minute I knew I was right.

"They never brought him up, you see." Jamie was still on the ground, just kneeling and not looking up at me. "I keep thinking that somewhere he's here, my dad and those other men. I know it isn't true, but I keep imagining they're still here, trapped and waiting for help."

I told Jamie that I guessed I knew, because I did, and then I turned and ran for home. I flew through my front door that evening and threw my arms around my papa and hugged him as hard as I could. All I knew was I didn't want to be Jamie Dawson for anything on earth.

I hadn't wanted to be Jamie then and I didn't want it now. As I helped Molly on that day of the cave-in, I kept repeating, "Let him be alive. Let them find him."

At some point that afternoon a storm blew up, with thunder, lightning, and heavy rain. The weather made the rescue attempt more urgent. A downpour could cause more caving in the tunnel. If the sump pumps had been knocked out by the cave-in, rainwater could flood whatever space the trapped men might have.

No one commented on the storm or even mentioned the rain.

Joe didn't come back for supper; none of the rest of us had much appetite, but we tried to act the same as usual.

When we were clearing up after the meal, Cliff asked quietly, "Betsy, do you want to go out a little later?"

I knew what he meant and nodded.

We didn't say so, but we gave the impression that we were going upstairs to study when we left the rest of the family in the living room. We put on our jackets, found flashlights, and slipped out the back door. The storm was making so much noise no one heard us leave. Cliff stopped by the shed to get a shovel.

"They have shovels," I told him.

"Not where we're going."

"Where are we going?"

He plunged off into the darkness and rain without answering. As we crossed the ridge behind the school, I glanced over toward the big, dark outline of the building and thought I saw a light moving past the window. I stopped for a moment and watched the light move, flickering past as though someone were walking, as we were, with a flashlight.

Realizing I was about to lose Cliff, I tore my eyes away from the school and ran to catch up. Only when we'd settled into a steady trot did Cliff answer the question I'd asked.

"The rescue team is working at the entrance to the shaft where the cave-in occurred." He spoke in spurts of words as we jogged along in the rain. "They're right.

That's the most likely place for the men to be. But just suppose they moved farther along the tunnel, suppose they heard the rumble and ran the other way. They could be near the other entrance."

"That shaft was abandoned because of a cave-in once before. The other entrance is blocked too," I reminded him.

No one had been hurt in the original cave-in at the Arcturus spur, but one entrance had been permanently closed.

Cliff nodded. "I know, but it's partly cleared. They just didn't finish because it isn't safe. I know it may not work, but I want to take a look."

I figured if Cliff's idea had been any good, the adults would have thought of it. Still, I had a lot of faith in Cliff; so I stuck with him. Twice I looked back over my shoulder, and both times I had the feeling that a light was following us. The goosebumps that ran up my arms weren't entirely from the cold and damp. The light from the schoolyard seemed to be chasing us up the hillside.

Uneasily, I plunged on, certain that whatever had been in the schoolhouse was now out in the storm with us.

When we reached the far side of the hill and the old entrance to the Arcturus spur, we started by pulling at loose rocks. The rain had softened the dirt around the rocks. Pebbles, rocks, and mud went sliding down as we scrabbled. That was the only help we got from the rain. We were soaked through by this time.

"There's a bit of an opening up here," Cliff told me. "Work your flashlight through it. If the men are in this end of the tunnel, the light should draw them this way."

I did as he said and, from then on, we relied on his flashlight and the lightning to see what we were doing. Somehow, I forgot the ghost light from the school.

One of my fingernails broke, and I could feel bloody cuts on both my hands. Cliff's shovel wasn't nearly as good as our own hands. I caught a glimpse of Cliff and knew how filthy I must be. We'd never keep this secret. Mama would just have to forgive us.

After a long while I sank back on my heels.

"It's no good," I shouted to Cliff. "We can't move that last rock; it's just too big. We're not going to get through."

Cliff continued to dig at the dirt around the rock.

"We can't quit now," he shouted back.

"This whole end of the tunnel could collapse when the last boulder is moved. We might be killing them!" My voice screeched above the storm.

Cliff shook his head. "This storm is going to collapse the tunnel anyway. If they aren't out of there tonight—" He didn't finish his thought. "We have to try. Help me with this rock once more."

I grabbed one side while he took the other and we tugged. The boulder was too big for us to get a grip on, and it was far too heavy for us—even together—to budge.

"We can't—" I began.

"Did you feel that?" Cliff interrupted.

I looked at him in confusion. "Feel what? It's too heavy for us."

"Someone's pushing!" he shouted. "I'm sure I could feel it. Here, try again."

I scrambled up and grabbed my side of the rock. Maybe Cliff was losing his mind, but I wanted him to be right. We grasped, pulled, slipped, got up, re-grasped, pulled, again and again.

There! I was sure I could feel it too. Someone was trying to help us from the other side.

But pushing wasn't going to release the boulder; more strength was needed on our side.

"We have to do it!" Cliff shouted, now out of sight on the other side of the large boulder.

I threw all my weight into trying to move that rock, and just then my foot slipped. I went sprawling, tumbling over loose rubble. Both legs stung from scrapes. I scrambled to get up and slipped again. I called to Cliff to wait for me, so he wouldn't waste his effort until I got back in place. The wind carried my words away.

"We have it now. That's great! Just keep doing what you're doing," Cliff yelled.

Once again, I called out to tell him that I wasn't there, but the rumble of loose earth and stones stopped me. I had to shift out of the way of falling rock. As the hillside finally released that giant boulder, Cliff and some dark figure both fell backward, sliding in the mud over loose stones. I didn't have time to think about the dark figure because just then a streak of lightning lit up the hillside revealing an opening where the old cave-in had been.

Forgetting my cuts and scrapes, as well as the mystery of who had been helping Cliff, I clawed my way forward just in time to see a man climb out through the opening.

"Where's the rescue team?" the first man out asked.

"On the other side of the hill," Cliff told him.

Two more men pulled their way through the opening, and then Papa came out.

Lightning struck again. Under cover of the roar of thunder, a different rolling boom began. The entrance, the one too dangerous to open, was closing once more in a slide of mud and rock.

All of us headed back over the hill. One of the four men from the cave-in had to be supported by two others. Slowly we struggled over the hill toward the entrance where the rescue team worked on.

We were shouting as we came over the hilltop, but no one heard us. No one needed to hear. A zigzag of lightning lit us up like figures on a movie screen. In the eerie, brilliant light that seemed to go on and on, I felt unreal. I looked down at the dirty, wet men at the foot of the hill staring open-mouthed up at us. Then I turned and behind us I saw one more figure, solitary and unmoving, outlined against the sky. I couldn't see a face, just a figure, with a flashlight in its hand. The lightning ended, darkness blotted out the landscape, and the men below began to move, running toward us. In the confusion and shouting that followed, I had no chance to mention what I had seen.

I didn't go to school the next day and neither did Cliff. Mama said that even if we weren't sick, we were half-drowned and exhausted. But it wasn't true. I felt full of energy, and my mind wouldn't slow down. I kept seeing everything that had happened, over and over again, lit up scene by scene in glimpses revealed by flashlight or lightning.

I told Cliff how I had been thinking about Jamie Dawson all the time after we heard about the cave-in, and Cliff said, "Yeah, and now Jamie's mama is dead too."

She had died a couple of months earlier, leaving Jamie with no one at all.

Oddly enough, when I slept, I didn't dream about the rescue. I dreamed instead about Billy Ray Bobble, who was running all around the school shouting, "I found the ghost! I found the ghost!"

By the time we went back to school on Monday morning, I had figured out the whole secret of the haunted schoolhouse. Well, it would be more accurate to say the secret had just come to me.

If you can't go through a door or a window, how else can you get into a school that's bolted and padlocked? And who would want to? I thought I had some pretty good answers, but I didn't intend to tell anyone except Cliff. I owed it to Cliff.

I told him what I wanted to do and he agreed to

come back to the school with me after dark. As it turned out, we had to wait until after everyone else went to bed. On this night no storm covered up the creaking of the staircase or the squeak of the back door. Still, we made it out.

By bright moonlight, we walked back to the school.

"I didn't think I'd ever want to break into this place."

"Do you think the principal left someone on guard?" I asked.

"I doubt it, but we don't want to take any chances."

We crept around the back of the building, circling bushes that looked like little grazing sheep in the light of the moon, working our way through a landscape that didn't seem much like the one we saw every day.

"I'll go first," Cliff said when we reached our destination.

"Here," I said. "Throw this down the chute before you go through."

He took the pillow from me, opened the flap for the coal chute, and dropped it through. Then he followed. When he called, "All clear," I slid down the chute too.

"So that much works," Cliff said, when we were both standing in the basement of the schoolhouse. "Where do you think he'll be?"

I didn't have an answer, but we climbed to the top of the basement stairs, opened the door, and waited to hear sounds.

It didn't take long. We found him in the home economics room, heating a can of soup.

"You have to wait really late to eat, don't you?" I asked.

"You two almost scared the life out of me," Jamie Dawson told us. "What are you doing here?"

"You can't stay here," I said.

"I don't have anywhere else."

"Your mother had a house," Cliff told him.

"A shack. Only there's no more heat or water or light. So a few weeks ago I started staying here overnight. It's not so bad. Look, you don't have to tell anyone, do you?"

So I told him what I wanted to do and how I thought it would turn out. We persuaded Jamie to go with us by arguing that we could bring fewer people in on his secret if we went to Papa and if we did it at night.

"Now, how do we get out of here?" Cliff asked. I'm not going back up the coal chute."

Jamie unlocked and opened a window, and the three of us jumped out into the bushes.

We picked ourselves up and headed for home.

Of course, just getting into our house brought a crowd of sorts. Mama and Papa got up, and so did Molly and Joe and James. Only Tommy and Cindy slept through the excitement.

Cliff and I told the story together, and Jamie took over at the end.

"I think this is a good time," I said at last. "Last

week everybody had a chance to think about how it would feel to be Jamie. He needs a place to live till he finishes school."

"I wouldn't mind working," said Jamie.

Mama and Papa talked it over. Molly had some suggestions, and so did Joe.

By the next day, Jamie Dawson was boarding with Mrs. Murphy, a high school teacher, who lived a block from the school. The location was convenient for Jamie's new job—night guard for the school, with responsibility for checking once a night to see that all was quiet and secure.

Apart from my family, only a handful of people ever heard the truth about the ghost in the schoolhouse or the mysterious figure who helped save four men from a cave-in.

Just before Christmas, I overheard someone asking Billy Ray Bobble about the ghost.

"That weren't no ghost," Billy Ray said. "It was just some squatter, but there won't be any more in this school 'cause now we got us a hired guard."

A
Dog
Named
Ransom

THE FIRST TIME HARRY NORTON ever saw Ransom, the dog was sitting up beside the driver on a mule-drawn wagon. Ransom sat up as high and was as black as the man; both of them rode straight with an easy, graceful sway.

Watching them, Harry decided that someday he'd own a mule and ride around with a big, proud-looking dog. He knew the man was coming to his house because his father had said he was hiring a man named Isaac to plow their back lot for them. Harry, who had never been shy, went out, introduced himself, and watched Isaac unhitch the mule.

"You gotta take her off the wagon every time you stop?"

Isaac gave a little shake before he answered. Or, maybe he was laughing.

"I got to unhitch her from the wagon so I can hitch her to the plow."

"She pulls your plow?" Harry, who was eight at the

time, was amazed. He had expected somebody to come and plow with a tractor. Machines of any kind were the gods of his world. He'd been looking forward to the tractor.

"I don't hold with automation," was all that Isaac answered.

Harry rolled the words around in his head a few times, and then tried them on his own tongue, but he couldn't match the ringing tone of Isaac.

When Isaac had unloaded the plow from the back of his wagon, Harry examined it, following with his hands the curving iron handles and the polished blades. He found the picture of a leaping stag.

"It has sharp blades."

"Almost as sharp as you. You run tell your dad I charge extra for nuisance."

"He's not here right now." Harry's father was an insurance agent who had an office downtown and also an office in his house. Most days he was downtown. "What's a 'nuisance'?"

"One kind of nuisance is having to give on-the-job training to pint-sized whippersnees."

Harry thought that over for a while. "You mean me," he said at last. "Am I really bothering you?"

"Not to say 'bothering,' no. But you could be a hindrance when I start to plow."

"Maybe I could just sit here with your dog while you plow. What's his name? Do you think it'll take you long?"

"Depends on how hard and rocky that field is—all

morning I'd guess. No, you can't sit with my dog, but you can introduce yourself. His name is Ransom, and he'll shake hands if you ask him nice."

Harry walked up, told the dog his name, and held out his hand. Ransom looked first at Isaac and then, when Isaac nodded, offered his paw.

"He shook my hand. Did you see that? Ransom shook my hand."

Isaac was now ready to plow.

"Look, Harry, you stay here on the shady side of the field. Each time I turn on this side I'll answer one question, just one!"

Harry nodded his agreement and trotted off toward the trees.

"Giddap! Go, Rosie. Giddap!"

As soon as Isaac was close enough to hear, Harry was ready with a question.

"How old is Ransom?"

"Be five in July."

Harry had to be satisfied with that until Isaac came back again.

"How old is the mule?"

"Rosie's eighteen. Old enough to vote."

"Don't you ever want a car?"

"Nope."

"What about trains? Everybody likes trains."

"I like 'em well enough, but they won't take me home, and I can't plow with one."

For every question, a furrow was plowed.

"Do you have any children?"

"I've got children and I've got grandchildren."

"What kind of dog is Ransom?"

"He's part shepherd and part Doberman pinscher."

"Why'd you name him 'Ransom'?"

"Why'd they name you 'Harry'?"

Harry had to wait until Isaac came back again to answer.

"I was named for my granddad."

"Ransom was named for a song."

When Isaac reached the shade the next time, Harry told him, "Someday I want to own a dog like Ransom."

"You own him, he won't be like Ransom. Me and Ransom's just friends."

All morning Isaac plowed with Ransom walking right beside him. At every turn on the shady side of the field, Harry asked a question.

By noon, his machine-gods weren't as secure in their heavens.

All that summer Isaac came from time to time to work in the garden. It seemed to Harry that Isaac's life must be just about perfect.

"Whatcha doin' when you leave here?" he asked one morning in August.

"Going fishing. I got a hankering for catfish to eat with a mess of greens."

"Do Ransom and Rosie go fishin' with you?"

"Sure do. I don't go anywhere Ransom and Rosie can't go. They have to wait outside, but they go to

CHILLS IN THE NIGHT

church with me too."

Harry wanted to go fishing with them but he didn't
ask. Some questions are easier to ask than others.

More than a year passed before Isaac invited him
to go fishing. In early spring of the year Harry was
ten, Isaac told Harry to walk along behind him as he
plowed and to pick up the worms that the plow
uncovered. Harry put some dirt into a plastic pail
and collected the worms that came crawling out
of the fresh-turned earth.

Harry went fishing with Isaac two or three times
that summer. Rosie would stand waiting in the shade,
and Ransom would lie on the bank beside them. At
the end of the day, Isaac would drive Harry home in
the wagon.

"Clean those fish yourself. A good fisherman doesn't
turn his catch over to anybody else."

Throughout the autumn and winter months,
Isaac delivered firewood in his wagon. And that's
how it happened that he knocked at the back door
one Saturday in December and asked Harry to
come outside.

"You hear that?" he asked, when Harry joined him
by the newly stacked wood.

From a distance came a raucous sound of honking.

"What is it?"

"You just stand and watch."

Eyes and ears straining, Harry stood beside Isaac and
Ransom and, like them, watched the sky. He saw it first
as just a black line in the sky. Then slowly it grew

into a deep V-shape. Finally, he could make out the individual birds that made up the flying formation. Long necks outstretched, heavy bodies moving high above him, the Canada geese were flying south and making a terrific racket.

"They give you plenty of warning so you can get out and see them. When that V passes straight over you and when you see them and hear them right above you the way we just did, that's good luck for a whole year."

Harry could feel the good luck. He and Ransom and Isaac were all going to have a good year.

"Superstition," Harry's dad said that night at supper. "Superstition is like a game. It can be fun, but you don't want to start believing it's real."

One day in the following summer, Isaac and Harry fished, and Ransom slept on the shady bank of the lake. Rosie cropped the grass while she waited to take them home.

In his sleep, the dog made noises deep in his throat. Occasionally, his feet made running motions.

"Think he's dreaming of a rabbit?" Harry asked.

"Yes and no. He's after something—could be a squirrel or a possum just as easy as a rabbit. And it isn't exactly a dream."

Harry had done some reading about dreams and about animal intelligence as well, but he had as much faith in Isaac's observations and beliefs as he had in scientific research.

"If it's not a dream—I mean a dream like people

have—what is it?"

"Out in the woods somewhere right now there's a real animal getting chased by a wraith of a dog. That animal's scared half out of his wits 'cause that great big something chasing him is Ransom's dream wraith."

Harry didn't comment. Most of Isaac's pronouncements weren't open to discussion. And, anyway, "dream wraiths" made as much sense as some of the articles he'd read.

That autumn Harry's dad hired Isaac to do some yard work: plant a tree, take out a row of shrubs, and clear the undergrowth from another section of hedge. Isaac was finishing up the work on a Saturday when the whole family was going away.

"Don't you worry," he told Mr. Norton. "I understand what you want."

When Harry's family came back around five in the afternoon, they saw that Isaac had started a small fire to burn the debris he'd cleared out of the hedge. On the top of the burning pile was the tree Harry's dad had left to be planted.

Mr. Norton, more baffled than upset, stopped the car in the driveway and hurried over, Harry trailing close behind. Ransom left Isaac's side and came running to meet Harry.

"Isaac, you're burning my tree. I wanted that cedar planted just where we took out the kids' swing set."

"I know you did, Mr. Norton, but I couldn't do that. If you look around behind the garage, you'll see

I planted a tree just where you wanted this one. I went out to the woods and I dug you up a nice big pine. It'll do right well for you there, and it's bigger than this tree."

"I didn't want a pine. I bought this tree, and it's the one I wanted you to plant."

Isaac was shaking his head. "I couldn't do that."

"Why? Why couldn't you do it?"

"If I'd planted that cedar tree, as soon as it grew tall enough to shade your grave, you'd die. I couldn't plant it, not knowing that."

Harry's dad argued a bit more, but there was no budging the old man. The tree was burning. He'd done what he had to do, and he'd do the same all over again if necessary.

"Superstition!" Harry's dad exclaimed in disgust. But the days passed, and he left the pine where Isaac had planted it. He didn't buy any more cedars.

Over the summers Isaac and Harry fished the creek, the lake, and the river. Little by little, Harry learned as much as the old man could teach him about fishing, and that meant Harry grew to be a very good fisherman. Isaac and Rosie and Ransom became part of the pattern of Harry's childhood. He thought they were a permanent part of his life, but he was wrong.

The four of them shared their last fishing trip the summer Harry was thirteen. At the time it just seemed like any other afternoon of river fishing. As usual, Rosie was in the shade. Ransom's great length was stretched out in the sun where he occasionally growled or stirred in his sleep.

"What do you think?" Harry asked. "A rabbit, a possum, or a squirrel?"

"It could be a skunk," Isaac said, laughing.

It was their last fishing trip because that was the summer somebody shot Isaac. He was killed right beside his wagon, and Rosie and Ransom were the only witnesses.

That year was a time in Harry's life when he was trying to act grown-up, and he listened to the details with all the detachment he could muster.

On a late Sunday evening, Isaac had driven his wagon into the alley behind the 600 block of Wilson Street. Apparently he had been out later than he had expected and had stopped at that particular place because there was an outdoor faucet where he could get water for Rosie before making the long ride out to his home in the country. He had picked the wrong time to stop. Grove's Liquor Store on Wilson Street was being burglarized. Police speculated that Isaac must have seen the burglar, who had broken in through the rear of the store from the alley.

Because he handled the insurance for the liquor store, Harry's dad knew all the details of the break-in/murder. Neither the robbery nor the murder would have been discovered before Monday morning if it hadn't been for Ransom. His howls had caught the attention of a passing patrol car. Rosie was hitched to the wagon; Isaac lay nearby with Ransom standing guard over him.

"Dad, I'd like Ransom to come live with us," Harry suggested.

"I don't know, Harry. Isaac's son is coming in from Chalmer's Mill today. He may want to keep Ransom."

"If he doesn't, could we take him? Would you ask?"

"Well, why not? I wouldn't want to see Ransom go to the pound, either."

Isaac's son sold Rosie and the wagon and was glad to accept the offer of a home for Ransom. And so it was that Ransom came to live with Harry and his family. Even though five years had passed since he first met Isaac, Harry still remembered their morning of questions and answers.

He had never forgotten that Ransom wasn't *owned* but was a friend. They had both been Isaac's friends, so Harry made up his mind that he'd be a friend to Ransom.

Ransom, by Harry's figuring, was now about ten years old, but the dog was still in his prime. Until Isaac's death, he had maintained a dignified friskiness. Now he looked to Harry as though he had changed somehow. The big, pointed ears still stood erect. His broad forehead gave a look of intelligence to his large head and his wide-set eyes. He rarely barked; but, when he did, the sound was a strong, bass rumble that shook the walls. He wasn't droopy or dejected-looking. Harry tried to analyze where the difference lay. Finally he decided there was something too alert about the set of the ears, too watchful about the eyes. Ransom didn't seem grief-stricken. He seemed to be a dog who was waiting, watching and listening, for something.

Maybe he thinks Isaac will come back, Harry thought. But after his friend was shot, the dog had stood guard. A dog as smart as Ransom must know that Isaac was gone for good. *So what is he waiting for?* Harry kept wondering.

Ransom settled in well to life with Harry's family. After a few days, Harry even persuaded the dog to sleep on the floor beside his bed. He began to hope that he might replace Isaac in Ransom's affections. Dogs are adaptable creatures. Ransom adapted, but he remained watchful.

One evening after supper, Ransom and Harry were keeping Mr. Norton company in his office at home while he waited for a client.

"I remember when I was just a kid and saw him for the first time. I thought he was part wolf. Isaac told me he's half German shepherd and half Doberman pinscher."

"He's a handsome creature," Mr. Norton acknowledged. "It's lucky that he's so gentle."

A knock sounded at the outside door to the office, and the hair along Ransom's back stood up straight.

"That should be Mr. Grove, the man whose liquor store was robbed," Harry's dad said, as he rose to open the door. "Come in, Gerald," he said to the man outside the door. "This is my son Harry, and his dog Ransom."

Like a tightly coiled spring, Ransom sprang to his feet; a growl rose menacingly.

"Easy boy. It's okay, Ransom." Harry caught the dog and spoke soothingly.

"I'm sorry about that, Gerald. He's usually a quiet dog."

Gerald Grove shifted uneasily. "He looks like a brute, not the kind of dog I'd like."

"A mutual feeling, obviously," Mr. Norton said lightly. "You'd better take him away, Harry."

Harry called, but Ransom stood his ground. He continued to bristle and alternated between vicious growls and high, hurt-sounding whimpers.

"Come on, boy," Harry demanded, catching Ransom's collar.

At last, Ransom gave ground; he turned his body while still fixing Mr. Grove in the glare of his huge, dark eyes. In a final snarl he showed his teeth. The sight of those fangs sent Mr. Grove backing up toward the door he'd just entered.

Harry tugged Ransom through the door at the opposite side of the room. As he turned to close it behind him, he saw a white-faced, trembling Mr. Grove.

"That dog's not safe," he was saying.

"Did you hear that, Ransom?" Harry asked the dog. "He doesn't think much of you. Why'd you have to go and act like that?"

Ransom was uneasy for the rest of the evening. As

Harry prepared to turn the dog out for his last run of the day, he hesitated, thinking how strange Ransom had been. As a precaution, he snapped a leash on the dog's collar and went out with him; but Ransom made an easy, loping circuit of the yard and came quickly back in.

As was now his custom, the dog settled down on the rug beside Harry's bed when the boy was ready to sleep.

Several hours later, Harry woke to the sound of soft growls and muted whimpers, typical noises of a sleeping dog, only louder and harder to ignore. Harry rolled to the edge of his bed, reached down, and stroked the dog.

"Good boy, Ransom. You must be after a real bear this time," he muttered sleepily.

Ransom's lip trembled and drew back in a snarl. A yip merged into a chest-rattling rumble.

"Easy, boy."

For several minutes Harry followed each growl with a reassuring pat. Then he slid off the bed and sat on the floor beside Ransom's head. He stroked the raised fur and kept repeating, "Easy. Steady. It's all right, Ransom."

And still the dog slept.

The red, glowing numerals on Harry's bedside clock said 3:45. Harry thought about waking the dog. Then vaguely he felt that it might not be a good idea. If touching him and speaking to him hadn't wakened him, maybe it would be too much of a jolt. *Like waking a sleepwalker*, Harry thought.

At four o'clock, he was still beside Ransom, speaking softly.

The dog was rigid with tension under Harry's stroking hands.

"You must be tangling with a grizzly," he said again.

Just watching the terrible struggle was tiring, but Harry was troubled and fought off sleep. Time and again the dog seemed to coil for some decisive spring; each time Harry concentrated all his energy on reassuring words and a gentle touch. Time and again he was relieved to feel the tension ease in the dog until the next surge of energy came.

Although Harry had no idea what was going on, it seemed like a death struggle. He could almost believe that each time he soothed the dog, he was pulling him back from some precipice.

Soon after five, Harry's head began to bob. He'd jerk into wakefulness every time his head dropped. Then he'd murmur something to the dog and stroke the big, furry shoulders. Finally, exhausted, he stretched out on the floor beside Ransom and fell asleep with one arm across the dog.

The next morning, Harry was stiff from his hours on the floor, but Ransom didn't seem any worse for his nightmares. In fact, he seemed filled with energy.

"Wrestling bears peps you up," Harry told him.

During breakfast, the phone began to ring. Harry's dad took the call and his end of the conversation was a series of startled monosyllables.

He left almost immediately without explaining the

phone call; but after Harry took Ransom out for a long run, he came home to find a message that his dad wanted to see him at his office downtown. Harry refused his mother's offer to drive. His dad hadn't said it was urgent; in fact, he hadn't said what it was about at all. Leaving Ransom in the house, Harry rode his bicycle into town.

Harry said "hi" to Mrs. Jacobs at the desk in the outer office, and she told him to go on through to see his father.

"Hi, son. Come in and take a seat," Mr. Norton called out.

He gave Harry a preoccupied smile that quickly faded.

"What's up, Dad?"

"Harry, Mr. Grove was banging on the sheriff's door around five o'clock this morning. When the sheriff opened up, Grove started babbling that he'd shot Isaac."

"Mr. Grove shot Isaac? But it was Mr. Grove's store that was being robbed!"

"According to what Grove blurted out at dawn this morning, there wasn't any real break-in. He said something about Isaac seeing him breaking his own back door after he had already emptied his office safe and taken dozens of cartons out of the store. At least, that was his first story."

"I don't understand. Why do you say his 'first' story? Did he shoot Isaac or didn't he?"

"He says now that he didn't, that his confession was

part of a nightmare experience."

"I don't understand."

"I don't understand either, son. But I think the best thing is for me to tell you Grove's whole story. He says that after he left our house last night he went back to his store where he worked on the books until the early hours of the morning. He claims the robbery hit him really hard, and he's struggling to hold things together until the insurance money comes through. That's why he came to see me yesterday evening; he wants to hurry things along.

"Anyway, he says that as he stepped out of his building to go home, he heard growls that sounded to him like a wild animal. He stood there pressed against the wall in terror until a 'huge beast' emerged from the shadows. He called it a great, black dog, but said it was more like a demon than a dog. For the next two hours he was at the mercy of this creature. He thought he would be killed and his body, like Isaac's, would be found behind his store.

"The dog apparently fastened itself onto his leg and dragged him, sometimes tossing him but always growling, until he was out of his mind with fear. He expected to be killed at any moment, but each time the dog seemed to move in for the kill it stopped short of mortal injury. The animal pulled him out of the alley and dragged him halfway through town before he loosened his hold.

"At that point, Grove ran for his life to the sheriff where he blurted out that first story about killing

Isaac. Now, he says that pure terror made him crazy and that he had nothing to do with the robbery and murder. And," Mr. Norton took a deep breath, "he's now demanding that the authorities send someone out to capture the dog. He claims he recognized it."

"You mean he thinks it was Ransom, don't you?" Harry said, suddenly realizing why his father had sent for him.

"Yes," his father agreed.

"Well, it wasn't. Ransom was beside my bed all night."

"Are you sure? He might have gotten out after you fell asleep, and it's a fact that he did take a real dislike to Mr. Grove."

"He woke me up in the middle of the night. He was growling, scrambling around in his sleep so much I couldn't sleep. Oh, Dad, that's it! Isaac told me dogs' 'wraiths' travel outside their bodies while they sleep. Ransom didn't chase Mr. Grove; his dream spirit did!"

"Nonsense!" Mr. Norton cried out, perhaps more harshly than he'd intended. He immediately added, "I know you valued your friendship with Isaac and so did I. But you can't believe the superstitious ramblings of an old man."

"At any rate, Ransom *didn't* leave my room all night. I finally lay down on the rug beside him. The two of us were there until breakfast time this morning."

"I think we'd better go tell that to the sheriff."

Harry and his dad went together to talk to the

sheriff. Careful not to mention dream wraiths, Harry
found he had plenty of reason to be grateful for the
nightmare that had cost him sleep but enabled him to
swear that Ransom had been by his side all through
the night.

"What will this mean to Mr. Grove?" Harry asked
his father that evening. "Do you think he'll still
blame Ransom?"

"I think Mr. Grove will have too many problems of
his own to worry about persecuting a dog."

"Do you think he's guilty? Won't the police believe
his confession no matter what he says now?"

"The police will be checking his whereabouts at the
time of the burglary, and his insurance payment will be
delayed. Even apart from the losses in the break-in, he's
in real financial difficulties. Yes, Mr. Grove has some
rough times ahead of him."

"Suppose he did rob himself, Dad. Why would he
do a thing like that?"

"Well, he needed money quickly. He could
have thought the insurance money would solve his
problem. *If* he robbed himself, he didn't really lose
anything, stock or money, and he stands to gain the
insurance money."

"I don't care about that. I just wish they'd find out
whether or not he killed Isaac."

The following morning word came that Mr. Grove
had shot himself while cleaning a gun. He was killed

instantly. The story of his experience with the dog-demon and his confession of murder had not been made public. So, as the news of his death spread, most people agreed that it was probably a tragic accident.

"I guess we'll never know the truth of it now," Mr. Norton said.

But it seemed to Harry that the truth was obvious. The proof of it was in the sudden change in Ransom. The dog lost his wary look. He seemed once again as carefree and playful as his dignity allowed.

"He feels at home now."

"He's finally adjusted to us."

"He just needed time to settle in," the other members of the Norton family said.

He avenged Isaac, and he knows it's over, Harry thought.

But he kept the thought to himself.

A
Plague
of
Crowders

"LOOK, MRS. NELLOP, I'm not responsible."
"No," she said thoughtfully and quite seriously,
"I daresay not. I've now taught five members of
your family and in my considered opinion there isn't a
responsible person among the lot of you."

Mrs. Nellop picked up the wastebasket and swept
the broken flowerpot – plant, dirt, and all – into it. It
might very well be that Jeff Crowder had not dropped
the potted plant onto her desk. But, even if he hadn't
done it himself, his actions had probably inspired it.

For almost a decade she'd had Crowders in her
history classes. Since she taught world history to the
eleventh-graders and American history to the twelfth-
graders and since the Crowders's sons were spaced at
two-year intervals, she hadn't been free of them for a
single year. But she was ready for this one, the fifth and
last of the lot.

Mrs. Nellop had been the librarian until Cal
Crowder, the oldest of the Crowders, stood up, picked

up his desk, and broke it over the head of Mr. Bain, the history teacher who had been attempting to explain Grattan's Parliament to his class.

It had been Mrs. Nellop's opinion that Cal Crowder should have been deported, possibly to Antarctica. But Mr. Cordwainer, the principal of the school, had said, "Boys will be boys, you know."

No, Mrs. Nellop did not know. "Just how am I expected to deal with boys who have already driven away three male teachers this year?"

"It's the opinion of the board," Mr. Cordwainer said, sheltering behind the Board of Education, "that you are the very best person to take on Mr. Bain's job. If anyone can restore peace and order to the history class, it will be you. We're counting on you, Mrs. Nellop."

That, of course, had happened a little less than ten years ago, and she had brought order to the classroom, though no one else had ever quite appreciated the price she had paid for that quiet, orderly room.

She had taken over classes in which students had known nothing—actually less than nothing because the things they thought they knew were all wrong. She still had some of those first tests she had administered. Asked about the American Civil War, five students had written essays about something they called the "Silver War" that Americans had fought against the British over taxes on cotton.

The students had learned nothing from those three teachers who had left battered, physically and mentally. They had learned nothing because until the advent of

Mrs. Nellop the history classes had been chaos.

"Where'd you get those shoes? I bet my dad would like a pair like that."

Those had been the first words Cal Crowder had said to her, earning him a quick laugh from the rest of the class.

Mrs. Nellop had responded to the challenge by taking the class step by step through the formation of the Irish Parliament and then assigning them an essay for the following day.

When Cal told her the next morning that he hadn't written an essay, she asked him to substitute an on-the-spot oral report.

With ladylike but biting sarcasm, she then reduced him to a laughingstock.

"You made a fool of me," he told her with rage after the class.

"I thought you enjoyed a good joke, Cal, and your knowledge of history is certainly a joke."

At five feet, one-and-a-half inches, Mrs. Nellop would never be physically imposing. But within a matter of days she was in complete charge of her classes. Her sharp wit and even the quirk of her eyebrow were to be feared.

She had a way of ducking her chin and raising her eyebrows while staring unblinkingly at anyone whose word or deed fell below her standards. Her look was fearsome. Her disapproval was terrifying.

Mr. Cordwainer and the board gratefully acknowledged that they had found a teacher who could "handle the problem students."

Observing the history classes, it was even possible to sympathize with the students. But that was only half the picture. In the middle of that first year, Mrs. Nellop had opened her door one Saturday morning to admit her cat Boswell. Boswell, however, had not been there to push past her, brushing against her legs, meowing to be fed. Mrs. Nellop began to search for Boswell. She hadn't looked far before she found the cat, quite cold and dead, left lying on her steps. He had been shot.

Mrs. Nellop didn't mention the matter to anyone. She didn't need to ask who had done the deed. She simply stored it away as over the next few years she would store away many things.

After Cal there had come Warren, Ted, and Martin, each one inspiring new outbreaks of classroom insolence. Mrs. Nellop had mastered them all, and had even taught them all a little history. She had not, however, been able to affect their characters.

After Boswell, she had not taken another pet, feeling that it wouldn't be fair to the animal, who might suffer a similar fate. The lack of pets to attack hadn't deterred the Crowders. They found other ways to plague her. Garbage was strewn across her front porch. Poison added to a birdbath left her a yard filled with dead birds. Once she had been prepared to leave for church when she found that her front door was blocked with rats and mice, all dead and many with the traps still attached. A plague of Crowders, that was how she thought of the Crowder boys.

Mrs. Nellop knew that the more harm you do to a person, the more you're inclined to despise that person. She was therefore fully aware that she was heartily abhorred by all the Crowders, who had been doing her harm and hating her for it for years.

"There's hope for every boy," Mr. Cordwainer would tell her from time to time. "They'll turn out to be fine young men. You'll see."

Mrs. Nellop had seen. She had followed the progress of all her former students and the Crowders were a bad lot. So far they had turned out to be loafers, layabouts, and troublemakers—when they found the energy for it.

The Crowders never forgot an imagined injury. So when Cal had graduated and been replaced by Warren, Cal and Warren had teamed up to plague her. When Ted became her student, he in turn was aided by both Cal and Warren in his efforts to harass her. Keeping track of the Crowders had never been a problem. Their interest in her had been cumulative. Now, this year, she had all five to face.

Fortunately, from Mrs. Nellop's point of view, the Crowders were predictable and gullible as well, which had allowed her to take some defensive action over the years. Their major campaign against her always came on April Fools' Day. By the time Ted, the third of the Crowders, had come along, Mrs. Nellop had begun to find ways to direct their malice. Near the end of March that year, she had hired someone to dig a flowerbed two feet wide and the full length of her front lawn. She then began to speak loudly and frequently at school about the rare and expensive bulbs that would soon be springing up in her yard. The ruse had worked. The Crowders had dug up her entire front yard, sifting through the dirt for bulbs. The rock garden in her backyard where she had in fact planted new bulbs was completely unharmed. Planted the autumn before, wild Asian tulips bloomed profusely among the stones. She reseeded the front lawn.

But such minor evasions were both inadequate and unsatisfactory. Mrs. Nellop was always aware that when it came to the Crowder boys, she was not living up to her own expectations of herself as a teacher.

During a long and busy lifetime, Mrs. Nellop had managed quite a few small miracles of transformation: churning cream into butter, turning lye and fats into soap, and changing curds and whey into cheese. Occasionally, she had even created a silky pursuer of knowledge out of a pigheaded teenager. But try as she might, she could not make a decent human being out of one of those five Crowder boys.

It was true, however, that any number of common transformations involve ingredients that in themselves aren't nice. It isn't pleasant, for example, to think that rennet, which is used in making cheese, is really part of a calf's fourth stomach.

And so, Mrs. Nellop began to think that if such not-too-nice ingredients as lye and fat—she always strained out all the impurities but fat was *fat*—could be made into pure, cleansing soap, then perhaps the

even less attractive Crowders might have the potential
to become something else. She had made it her
work to find a formula and to search out just the
right additional ingredients to bring about the
transformation.

The formula had been found only after years
of looking. (Mrs. Nellop took her responsibilities as a
teacher very seriously.) It was so old that it was called
a "receipt," which is an old-fashioned spelling of
"recipe." Still, Mrs. Nellop told herself, a formula for a
successful transformation would be as sweet whatever
name it might be called.

The preparations had taken more than a year. She
had found herself hunting down a number of very odd
things, hairs from the underbelly of a nursing sow, for
instance. Neatly clipped, bottled, and labeled "Bristle,"
the hairs achieved a sort of dignity. Forty-three
ingredients in all she had collected, only having to
guess at one or two of them. (She hadn't been at all
sure what the Palimenox plant was, for example.)
Some, of course, had required additional treatment
after they had been found. She pickled turtles' eggs,
soured rabbit's milk, toasted nasturtium seeds, which
are so tiny she could hardly say if, in the end, they
were toasted, burned, or merely singed.

But finally in March of the last year of the
Crowders, she was ready to deal with them. As she had
done with some previous success, she began to direct
attention toward a particular focus for mischief. One by
one, she brought small, heavy crates into her classroom,

depositing them with an air of eager anticipation.

"What a treat we'll have next month!" she'd say.

"What is it, Mrs. Nellop?"

"You must wait and see," she told her classes, making sure Jeff Crowder heard. "We must be sure to keep all these things safe and *separate* from each other until next month. Oh, if they should be mixed, what a disappointment that would be!"

The last of the boxes was added to the collection on March 31, and Mrs. Nellop surveyed the stack with satisfaction. She had done her best. She had made sure everything necessary was available. The rest was up to the Crowders. A teacher, after all, can only do so much. The last steps must always be taken by the students.

With good fortune that seemed more than fortuitous, April 1 fell on a Saturday, allowing both time and freedom to those who wished to play elaborate April Fools' jokes.

When Mrs. Nellop arrived at school the following Monday, she found that someone had broken into her classroom. To the group of students in the hall, she appeared very calm. If anything, she looked faintly pleased.

She pushed against the door in its splintered jamb and stood for a moment gazing into the room. Every one of those sturdy little crates had been smashed. At first glance, all the onlookers saw were the shattered remains of the cases. Next, they noticed that in one corner of the room the desks had been pushed back to make space for an old bathtub that had clearly been brought there for the purpose of mixing together all the contents of those numerous packages.

Only after all the wreckage had been noted, did someone catch sight of the large black bird perched above the chalkboard. Above the window was another, on top of the roll-up maps another, above the door through which students now crowded another, on the bookcase at the back of the room a fifth one.

"Crows?" Mrs. Nellop said wonderingly. "How surprising. Perhaps the pickled eggs have gone bad."

She asked some of the students to open the windows and shoo the birds out, which proved difficult and time-consuming. But at last the five birds were outside, scattered among the still-bare branches of a tree, staring in at the students who stood at the windows staring back.

"Who do you think did this?" someone asked.

And someone else gave the obvious answer, which seemed confirmed when Jeff Crowder failed to show up for classes that day.

In the following days he continued to stay away and the rumor slowly spread that all the Crowder sons had left town.

"Unexpected," commented Mrs. Nellop, "but not unsatisfactory." And everyone assumed she was referring to the sudden departure of the town's troublesome boys.

Of course, the thing hadn't turned out precisely as she had intended. A fault in that old "receipt," perhaps? Some inaccuracy in her measurement of ingredients?

Or, more likely, something in the composition of the Crowders that she had failed to take into consideration. Well, in any case, she couldn't count it a failure.

It is a primary duty of a teacher to help her students become productive citizens of the world. If it is impossible to turn some of them into worthy citizens, then perhaps useful denizens of the air is not a bad alternative. Unpleasant though crows may be, no one would deny that they do serve a useful purpose in nature's scheme of things.

These days Mrs. Nellop often steps out her front door to see five haughty crows ranged among the topmost branches of the fir tree in her front yard waiting, as crows do, for a chance to apply themselves to clearing away the remains of animals unfortunate enough to fall victim to the day's highway traffic.

Mrs. Nellop always nods to them pleasantly and sets off briskly to another day of remolding this year's flock of students.

A
Game
of
Statues

"I DOAN HAB A CODE! My doz is 'tuffy. Thad's awd
it idz."

Silently, Brian watched the red-haired boy plead
with his classmates to let him join their game of storm-
the-castle.

"Get lost, Tommy. Nobody wants your old 'code'!"
shouted the one called Mark.

Brian quickly turned away before Tommy could
notice him. *Better to be on my own than stuck with a creep
my first day in a new school,* he told himself.

Brian was an old hand at adjusting to new schools.
He had moved seven times in the last two years. With
all that experience, he had developed basic rules for
settling into a new place. He was never in a hurry to
be friendly. He took his time sizing up a class. The
important thing was to spot the leader.

It was easy to spot the leader here. Mark was clearly
the most powerful boy in the class. You'd never catch
Brian begging to join in a game like that Tommy had.

No, Brian knew a better way. The first couple of days would be tough, but he had learned to be patient. By the end of the week, Mark and the rest would be begging to play his game.

Watching from the schoolroom window, Mrs. Whitman shook her head. She saw Tommy Humphreys turn away in dejection. She waited to see if Tommy and the new boy would team up. They didn't. The new boy wasn't trying to join the others' game, she noted. Some of the boys should have asked him. She'd have a private word with Mark after school. Brian appeared content on his own, but the others should have tried to make him feel welcome.

The April afternoon passed slowly in the classroom. Asked to read aloud from *The Classic Stories Anthology*, Brian read clearly and with no appearance of shyness. When Mrs. Whitman asked Tommy to explain a math problem from the homework assignment, he flushed to the roots of his red hair and said, "I habn't got id done."

A snicker of contempt started from Mark, who held his own nose and said, "He didden hab tibe to do id!" The snicker spread through the class.

Odd, Mrs. Whitman thought. She had never before noticed that Mark was so unpleasant.

The next day, clouds darkened the morning sky. Before the first recess rain had begun to fall in sheets, lashing the windows and blotting out the world outside.

During the break from their schoolwork, the students played with marbles or jacks in the hall outside the classroom or stayed at their desks and talked. Except for Brian. Brian sat at his desk reading until the class began again.

At lunch Mrs. Whitman spoke to her friend Mrs. Ames, who taught the other fifth-grade class.

"Of course it's hard to tell with a new student. He seems to be adjusting well, but he simply has nothing to do with the others. And since he came," she added, rushing a bit now that she'd gotten around to her real worry, "the others seem different."

"How do you mean 'different'?" Marge Ames asked her friend.

"Oh, not as easygoing as they used to be." Somehow she couldn't bring herself to say that the class, which she had liked well enough last week, now seemed to be made up of unpleasant and unlikable children. Except for Brian.

Mrs. Whitman had allowed them thirty minutes to finish filling in the blanks in the exercise assigned in their social studies workbook. Brian had finished in seven minutes, but he pretended to continue working, looking up occasionally to study one or another of his classmates. Joey and Harold looked like twins and acted like twin servants to Mark. They weren't really related, Brian knew; but their blond hair combed just alike and their devotion to Mark made them seem like bookends.

Brian's glance slid past Tommy to where Carl was chewing the end of his pencil and staring blankly at his workbook. He wouldn't finish the assignment, and it wouldn't matter because everything he did was wrong anyway. The next time Brian looked up he sought out Mike, a serious boy who probably had more brains than Mark but who let himself be led around like a sheep.

Brian sighed and turned a page in his workbook. It was always the same. More than anything he wanted friends; he wanted to be a part of it all—the games, the jokes, the roughhousing. And it would work too, if only he could just walk into a school and be one of the gang instantly.

It's the waiting that ruins it, he thought. *Once you start to watch them, it's all spoiled.* He looked again and saw Tommy surreptitiously wiping his nose on his shirt sleeve. Brian dreamed of having a boon companion, not a drippy follower who would latch onto him because nobody else would play with him.

Just for an instant, he pictured himself balanced on a log over the creek jousting with Mark. Brian shook his head, chasing away the picture. Mark wouldn't do for the kid in his dream any more than Tommy would. Brian's best friend couldn't be a bully, a whiner, a copycat, or a sheep. He scanned the room again, ignoring the girls. No, taking a look at people spoiled them for you. Mrs. Whitman called time, and Brian shrugged. It was okay. He would play with them anyway. Sometime soon.

In a sudden spring chill, the town was gripped
with frost that night. And there was talk on the
weather report of another late snow in the offing. Mrs.
Whitman noted that the spring clothing had been put
aside the next day. The children came to school with
warm sweaters covered by their heavy jackets. All
except Brian.

At recess time she called him aside to ask if he
would be warm enough.

"The cold doesn't bother me," he told her.

"If you feel chilled, you can come and stay in the
room. We can't have you out there freezing."

He smiled at her, a fleeting expression that went
straight to her heart and made her think again, *What a
nice child he is!*

Mrs. Whitman made up her mind to cut recess short
that Wednesday. No sense in letting the kids catch cold.
From her vantage point at the classroom window, she
watched them. Within minutes, some of the girls began
to return, taking up games inside the building rather
than facing winter's last blast. *Perhaps I should call them
all back in now,* Mrs. Whitman thought. But she stopped,
her attention caught by the scene outside.

The two opposing teams in storm-the-castle were
slowly being killed off. As they "died" in battle, the
boys left the game one by one. Today there were several
of them wandering around, left out of the final battle.

A stupid way to play any game, Brian thought. But in
all his various schools, he'd had a chance to see lots of

different leaders. Letting people drop out of a game, or making them drop out, was a mistake plenty of leaders made. It was a mistake Mark was making. So far Mark had just ignored Brian. Mark, as the established leader here, was so sure of himself that he was confident the new kid would eventually come to him asking to join a game, if not this one the next one. Brian knew exactly what was going on in Mark's head. He knew because he had known so many kids like Mark, not that all leaders were alike. Mark belonged to the "bully-organizer" category of leader, the ones who take charge by pushing people around and always having plenty of ideas of what to do next. He scared them, and he kept one step ahead of them. But not ahead of Brian.

Everybody who was not a part of Mark's game had gathered in a knot at the edge of the playing field. It was time to make a start, time for Brian to make a move.

"What'll we do?" somebody asked.

"Statues," Brian answered clearly and firmly before discussion could start. "We'll play a game of statues."

For a wonder, nobody bothered to say, "That's kids' stuff!" In fact, they didn't even seem to know the game. Brian had to explain.

"That's all there is to it," he said, when he had covered the rules. "The way we'll play though is that nobody drops out. If the Master of the Game catches you moving, he'll just cast his eye on you and freeze you. You'll be a statue for the rest of the game."

"What if somebody gets caught but still tries to

sneak forward to win?" Joey asked. "*I* think we ought to put people out when they're caught moving."

"I'll be Master of the Game," Brian said. "You won't move after I catch you."

"Aw, heck, let's give it a try."

Mark's game of storm-the-castle had used the bleachers beside the playing field as a castle. As the last of the victorious knights straggled back across the field, they were startled to see all the losers from their game spread out over the lower half of the field, some standing poised for movement holding very still and others seemingly frozen in the middle of motion. Joey had both arms flung out, one knee raised high in the air as though leaping and only one toe touching the ground. He looked as though he would fall over if you tapped him. Carl seemed to have fallen already and was resting on the toes of both feet and the tip of his nose, with arms raised toward the sky above his back.

Mark and his last surviving knights raced toward them in astonishment. Just before they reached the group, Brian called out, "Game's over. We'll play again tomorrow."

"What's going on here?" Mark asked.

Nobody answered him.

Harold grabbed Joey's arm. "How could you freeze like that?" he asked him.

"I don't know. It felt really strange."

"He didn't catch *be*," Tommy bragged through his stuffy nose.

CHILLS IN THE NIGHT

But no one was interested in who hadn't been caught.

"When the Master of the Game turned and saw me moving, it felt like ice crystals formed all through me. I couldn't have moved a fraction of an inch," Mike explained.

"Well, I don't know how to describe it, ice crystals or what," Carl said, "but I did feel sort of like a snowman or something."

"Snow*ball*, you mean," Mark said, still trying to take charge of the conversation, but it was too late. They were back at the classroom.

On Thursday, the predicted snow still hadn't come, though the temperature stayed near freezing.

Mrs. Whitman warned, "Let's enjoy outdoor recess while we can. Tomorrow we may have that snowstorm and not be able to get out at all."

This recess, all the boys joined in the game of statues. Mrs. Whitman watched as the various players tried to creep toward the master. Mark seemed especially determined; he clearly wanted to win the right to become the master himself. But Brian was quick. Some of the boys shuffled forward constantly when Brian's back was turned, but he could whirl with astonishing speed and catch them. Some of the boys stood very still and then dashed forward. Brian seemed to sense the very moment they started to move. The strange thing was the way they stopped. Oh, the ones who weren't caught looked normal enough. But, when

Brian caught someone moving, that person froze in midair, holding the pose like a real statue.

In spite of herself, Mrs. Whitman felt contempt for the players' clumsy efforts against Brian. She reminded herself that her boys were ordinary students just like the ones in every class she had taught: a pair of friends who wanted to be just alike, a leader who was a bit of a bully, a bright boy who lacked confidence, a stuffy-nosed kid who whined. They were just boys like any others, but something had happened to her sympathy for them.

I'm seeing them from an outsider's point of view, she thought. She looked again at Brian and shivered. The cold, like her new view of her students, seemed to have come with Brian.

When recess ended, no one moved until Brian called an end to the game. Since no one had managed to reach him, he was still Master of the Game. The boys came in grouped in twos and threes, talking, almost gasping out their sense of adventure, eyes wide with excitement. All except Brian, who came in as quietly as usual.

The game hadn't looked that exciting, but the players seemed to feel they'd had a wild and dangerous outing.

During the afternoon, Mrs. Whitman asked them to write a story, a story with a snowy setting, she specified, eyeing the snow clouds thickening outside. In the last hour of the schoolday, she had the fifth-graders read their stories out loud.

Brian had written a story about a snow king's garden. Purple, gold, and white crocuses pushed through the snow in the king's garden, and every day he went out to admire the flowers, but the flowers begged to be picked and made into a bouquet. Day after day the king refused. Finally, he couldn't resist their pleas any longer. He picked them, put them all together in a bowl, and brought them into his castle. The next day all the flowers had wilted.

Brian's story seemed to chill the room. The listeners felt that they were bright petals, pushing out through a crust of snow to stand trembling under the spring sun.

When Brian finished his story, the class sat silent. Mrs. Whitman sat silent too, thinking it a strange story for a ten-year-old to write.

Mark snapped out of the spell of the story first.

A little angrily, he said, "Snow kings and crocuses! That's dumb!"

Mrs. Whitman stepped in quickly to offer positive comments. Mark had never seemed so rude before these last few days.

Mrs. Whitman was always delayed a few minutes after school was over, straightening the room and preparing for the next day. When she left that afternoon, she was surprised to see that the boys from her class were still outside the building. They appeared to be continuing their game from the morning recess, all of them in staggered lines playing at being statues. All except Brian, who was still Master of the Game.

She was cooking her supper at home when her phone rang the first time.

"Carl isn't home. Do you know where he might be?" her caller asked.

As soon as she had finished talking to Carl's mother, Joey's mother called.

"Joey didn't come home from school. I've talked to Harold's mother and he isn't home yet either."

When Mark's father called next, Mrs. Whitman decided that she had better go over to the schoolyard as she had directed the parents to do. During the day when the weather was fair, it was possible to see the field behind the school from her back porch. But now it was night—and a night made even darker by clouds.

As she reached the school grounds, she could hear parents shouting. Just then someone turned on the lights for the playing field, and in the sudden brightness she saw the boys from her class. They were standing still as statues, frozen into the oddest postures. She moved quickly among them, checking them against a mental roll. Yes, they were there, all of them. All except, of course, Brian.

Ghost
of
Christmas
Past

MY GREAT-AUNT MOLLY HARDISON was a wealthy woman. By the standards of the coal-mining town that was home to my family, she was fabulously rich. We didn't have any particular claim on her; she had nearer relatives. Still, she never forgot us children—and there were eight of us—at Christmastime. Once in every two or three years, she would come and spend the holiday with us.

Mama said that Christmas with us was more like Aunt Molly's childhood holidays than Christmas at her own house or with her sons and their snooty wives.

We were poor all the time, and some years were poorer than others. Still, at Christmas our house would be filled with evergreen boughs, pinecones, and red ribbons. Mama would keep hot cider simmering on the back of the woodstove so the house always smelled of cinnamon and cloves. No matter how bad things were, Papa could take his hunting dog and bring in game. When I was very young the dog was Ol' Elsie, and then later Papa hunted with Elsie's son Ol' Ben. Papa brought home quail by the dozens, deer, and wild turkeys.

Sometimes he'd be the only person we knew who had found a turkey, but he'd always get ours for the holiday. I think he was smart in the ways of turkeys. I was his tomboy and counted myself in on his discussions about hunting with my brothers. Papa would follow a good-sized turkey gobbler for weeks, learning its ways and finding its roosts. Turkeys like to move around, which is why they fool so many hunters, and they almost always have more than one roost.

I listened to all my father could tell us about hunting and would have gone with him when he began to take Joe and Cliff, but Mama put her foot down. I had to content myself with taking care of the hunting dog.

"Maybe someday, Betsy," Papa consoled me. "You'd make a fine hunter."

In any case, our house looked and smelled good at Christmas. It was filled with all the food a resourceful country family could provide. In our neck of the woods that was better than most city families, poor or rich, could do.

So fairly regularly, Aunt Molly would come and spend Christmas in our bustling, overcrowded house. Whether she was there or not she always sent presents. Her sister, our own grandmother, was dead, which made her something of a stand-in. But we children understood that presents for Christmas and our birthdays would be all we could expect from Aunt Molly, barring my sister Molly.

I don't think any scheming was involved on my mother's part. I think she just liked the name "Molly." She named her first daughter for her mother and her second daughter for her aunt. It didn't hurt that both Mollys happened to be green-eyed redheads. Our Molly was the only redhead among the eight of us and the only one with green eyes. We understood, all of us from oldest to youngest, that our Molly was special to Aunt Molly.

Aunt Molly made it clear that something more than seasonal presents would come Molly's way. I was five and my sister Molly was twelve the Christmas when Aunt Molly first brought her ruby and diamond necklace with her.

"It isn't yours yet," Aunt Molly told my sister Molly, "but it will be. I'm not having it go to either of my daughters-in-law. It'll be yours."

We were all in awe of those old stones that glowed with life. Even the boys took a look, rolled their eyes, and murmured, "Wowee."

"When?" my sister Amanda, oldest of all and most practical, asked.

Aunt Molly fairly cackled.

"When? Well, you see, she'll get to keep it when she marries. Marriage," Great-Aunt Molly said, "is a better milestone than age eighteen or twenty-one."

From then on, every Christmas that Aunt Molly

spent with us included another look at the necklace
and another review of when Molly could claim it.

When my sister Amanda was nineteen, she married
Dr. Harvey Brittaman, a young general practitioner,
who had just opened an office in our area. Great-Aunt
Molly gave Amanda and her husband a full set of fine
dishes, 102 pieces.

Everybody agreed that none of the rest of us girls
was likely to do any better than Amanda had. After all,
a doctor!

Sister Molly was seventeen that year. I always
thought she was the best-looking of all of us, though
later on my little sister Cindy turned out to be a
beauty too. Molly had creamy fair skin without freckles
and deep dark-red hair. She was slim and tall and wore
her hair long. She liked nothing in the world better
than reading and carried a book with her everywhere.
She would sit on a damp hillside and read until
someone found her and told her to come home.

She had lots of admirers in high school, but
two were the frontrunners. Malcolm Bodey was a
football player and Jerry Rattagan edited the school
newspaper. Malcolm was planning to go into the
mines like the rest of his family. Jerry was going on
to the state university.

"You wait for the older men," Aunt Molly told sister
Molly when she came for Amanda's wedding. "These
boys are fine, but someone better will come along."

That wedding started me thinking. I was ten at
the time. I thought about losing Amanda. I thought

about marrying in general. I thought about me. I tried to picture marrying one of the boys I knew, and it was an awful thought. I decided to try again to persuade Mama to let Papa teach me to hunt. I figured what I'd really like was to be a woodsman and live alone in a cabin in the woods. In our house I never had any time or any place alone.

Then I thought about Molly, Molly and the ruby and diamond necklace. For the first time I saw that the necklace hadn't been anything but trouble. For one thing, it had turned my sister Amanda bitter. Here she was the oldest and the first married, but she wasn't getting the necklace. Aunt Molly had given her Royal Doulton china worth a king's ransom, but it didn't take away the sting. Amanda bore the brunt of the sense of rejection, but I suddenly saw that it was there for all of us, boys as well as girls.

A year later Molly graduated from high school and went to work at Lacy's drugstore. She didn't talk to any of us about what she wanted, but it was easy to see she was unhappy. Malcolm was determined to marry her, and it seemed to me she was weakening.

I felt like there was something about Molly I was missing, so out on the hillside one day I just asked her outright, "How do you really feel about that necklace Aunt Molly's going to give you when you get married?"

Well, she told me. I guess nobody had ever asked her that question before. She spilled out her feelings, her hopes, her wishes—everything in one long outburst.

"Didn't you know?" she asked me. "Didn't you guess? You're the one who's always watching everybody. I thought you didn't miss a thing—not that I expected anybody else to guess. But I thought you would."

I felt pretty stupid. Once she told me, it seemed obvious.

That next Christmas was one that Aunt Molly spent with us. She showed up two days before Christmas, in time to put her presents under the tree and to help with some of the cooking. Her coming brought back all the things I'd been thinking about when Amanda was married. When you're eleven-going-on-twelve, you're plagued by a lot of thoughts.

My brother Cliff was the one person in the family I always confided in, but he'd picked that moment to have a chest cold or flu of some sort. He had been moved into the little room at the head of the stairs that was used as a sickroom whenever Mama suspected one of us had something contagious. We were only supposed to pass notes to each other, sending them in on the food trays.

I put up with my serious thoughts all on my own for as long as I could, then went and knocked on the sickroom door.

"Who is it?" If a toad had a voice, it might sound all croupy like Cliff's that day.

"It's Betsy. I'm coming in."

I went down to the far end of the bed and sat by Cliff's feet. He didn't say you shouldn't be here. He just said, "I can't talk so good."

"Well, you can listen." And I told him all the things I had thought about marriage, about the necklace, and about Molly. While I was talking, some things that had never entered my mind before seemed clear. Cliff croaked that since he wasn't the marrying type and I wasn't either, maybe we could both be hunters.

I felt a lot better after that. I wasn't weird after all. I slipped out of his room before Mama showed up with his lunch.

After supper that night we all gathered in the parlor. Cliff, his chest wrapped with flannel cloths that smelled of camphor, was bundled into a chair by the fireplace, Ol' Ben asleep at his feet. Even Amanda was with us. Her husband Harvey Brittaman was there too; but the two youngest children didn't know that because Dr. Brittaman was dressed as Santa Claus and carried a big bag of toys.

He distributed presents and we all opened them. In the morning we would open the ones from under the tree. We liked to spread Christmas out as far as we could.

Christmas Eve was always the time Aunt Molly asked Molly to wear the ruby and diamond necklace, "for a while, so I can see it on you, child." Aunt Molly laid it out on the table, and we all saw that it was still as impressive as ever. It seemed to catch the lights of the Christmas tree and the glow of the candles, not only reflecting but matching with light of its own.

Just as Aunt Molly said, "Come here, my dear, and let me put this necklace on you," Cliff had a fit of coughing. Everyone's attention turned from the necklace to Cliff.

Aunt Molly laid down the necklace and stood up to look over the back of Cliff's chair. One younger child climbed on each arm of the chair, Cindy on one side and Tommy on the other. Harvey Brittaman, who was a doctor first and Santa second, tossed his sack to one side and trotted across the room in his black overshoes. Someone tramped on Ol' Ben's tail, and he yelped. I led the dog toward the front door.

"Cliff's all right," Papa said. "Don't open that door," he added to me. "I don't want a draft through here while Cliff's downstairs."

I slapped Ol' Ben on the bottom and sent him off to his box in the kitchen.

The little ones scrambled back to their presents. Aunt Molly, with a hand pressed to her bosom, turned back to the table. Mama picked up a bottle of cough medicine and almost dropped it as Aunt Molly screamed.

"Who picked up the necklace? Molly, do you have it already?"

Looks of bewilderment met her questions. "Don't go out!" she commanded Santa Claus, who was trying to slip out the door with his empty sack to change back into his identity as Dr. Brittaman. "Don't anyone move out of this room until I find the necklace."

"You can't suspect Santa Claus!" my brother James shouted, which was a cue for silly chatter from the rest of the kids that had a bad effect on Aunt Molly's temper. As a result Aunt Molly was much more thorough and more demanding in her search than she might have been otherwise.

Mama and Papa kept trying to make light of it. Of course, the necklace was there. It had to be. None of us would take it. Aunt Molly said she would have granted that an hour earlier but the fact was someone had taken it or else the house was haunted.

Our Santa Claus suggested we quarter the room and search it inch by inch with Aunt Molly supervising each stage of the search until the necklace turned up. That search was classic, something to pass into legend within our family. First, there were twelve people in the room, counting Aunt Molly herself; and someone insisted she should not be exempt from being searched. Santa and his sack were checked. Even Cliff agreed to be searched, his chair, his blankets, his clothes, his flannel wraps, every inch of the space around him.

Every branch of the tree was examined, every present inspected for signs of tampering. Two of them had to be opened and then rewrapped because young hands had been scrabbling at them. But neither one contained the necklace. Chairs were overturned. The hanging light fixture was checked. It became a game to suggest new possibilities.

Maybe because he had been caught trying to get out the door, Harvey Brittaman went to extremes to see that he and his Santa props were cleared of suspicion. He also made sure every suggestion, no matter how unreasonable, was followed up. The windows were tested, even though everyone knew no one had opened a door or a window. An icy wind was blowing and it was snowing outside. Opening up just long enough to toss something out would have let in a blast of cold air that everyone would have noticed, not to mention that the necklace would have been lost in the snow.

No possibility was overlooked. The rubies couldn't be gone, but they were. The impossible had happened, and our living room felt haunted that night.

Aunt Molly had never seemed the least bit pitiful to anyone before that night. Now she looked like a broken woman. Her face was blotchy and her shoulders sagged. I felt truly sorry for her. Like everyone else that night, I wanted to give her necklace back to her, but it just wasn't possible.

Mama put her arm around Aunt Molly and told her she'd walk her up to her room. At the living room door, Aunt Molly turned and, looking at Molly, said, "I'm sorry, dear."

"We'll find it," Mama told Aunt Molly. "We'll still find it."

Papa, Amanda, and Dr. Brittaman were all shaking their heads behind Mama and Aunt Molly. I knew what they were thinking. That necklace had just plain vanished, and it didn't seem likely it could ever be found. If it wasn't in that room, well, where could it be?

Papa carried Cliff back to his bed. The rest of us also began to get ready to go to sleep. No one knew quite what to say to Molly.

We shuffled through nighttime rituals in uneasy silence. This was no way to go to bed on Christmas Eve. Aunt Molly was hurt; and to all appearances, we had a thief in our family. A dull misery settled around my heart.

You wouldn't think a holiday could recover from a disaster like that, but the next day was one of the best Christmases of our lives. Strangely enough it was all due to Aunt Molly. Several times during breakfast I saw her fingering a small piece of folded paper. She opened her presents with the rest of us and sounded sincerely grateful for her box of handkerchiefs, bottle of toilet water, book of poetry, plus the handmade gifts from the younger children. If she grieved, she did it privately. It seemed to me she just looked thoughtful.

In the middle of the afternoon, when the younger children were playing and Amanda and Harvey Brittaman had gone home, Aunt Molly said she had something to say. She gathered Mama and Papa and Molly around the table. I hung around to hear what was going on.

"I've been doing some thinking since last night," she told them. "No, don't interrupt," she cautioned as my mother began to speak. "I think I wanted to arrange for my namesake to have my life all over again, a thing that's not possible, not even reasonable." She stopped and sighed.

"It's all right about the necklace. I mean, it isn't all right that you lost it," Molly told her. "But it's all right that it isn't coming to me."

Aunt Molly ignored her and continued, "I'd like to see this young woman go on with her studies. Toward that end, I want to pay her way to college."

At a sign of protest from my father, Aunt Molly said dryly, "Believe me, four years' tuition will be less than the value of that necklace. You will not, of course, get the necklace," she added to Molly.

"Thank you," said Molly, her eyes wet and shining.

Molly walked on air for the rest of the day. Aunt Molly beamed. My parents kept exchanging smiles. The rest of us were infected by their joy, so it felt like Christmas morning all day and half the night.

I worked it out the other day that Aunt Molly on that Christmas was about the age I am now. I, of course, am not old at all, although she seemed old to me then. She just recently died, having lived into her nineties. Her estate was divided among her children and grandchildren, but her will made provision for a sealed manila envelope to be delivered to me.

When I opened the envelope, I found a correctly folded letter on thick creamy stationery together with a yellowed slip of paper folded into a square. I opened the slip of paper first and read the message:

You can have you mizerable neclace back if you promise Molly don't haf to get married. She don't want a husban. She wants to go to collige.

I wouldn't have believed the spelling could have been that bad. I unfolded the accompanying letter and read:

Dear Betsy,

I don't know how many years will pass before you get this back, but I want to return your note to you.

For days I was baffled by the disappearing stunt you pulled. "No one had left the room yet the necklace wasn't in the room," I told myself. Continuing to puzzle over the problem, I repeated that paradox endlessly. Finally, I varied it a bit and said, "Not one creature went out of the room." I stopped as I reached that point, because I realized a "creature" had left—that smelly old hound. Then I knew my ruby and diamond necklace must have gone out of the room with the dog. He was wearing it there in his box by the kitchen stove all the time we were searching, wasn't he? Of course, I also remembered that you were the one who sent the dog out of the room while Cliff kept the rest of us distracted. What a determined child you must have been to hold out against all that adult energy!

You always were a clever child, Betsy.

Aunt Molly had gone home that year with her necklace. Late on Christmas afternoon, it showed up without explanation on her bed. She made sure everyone saw it one last time, then after that holiday never mentioned it again.

When the new semester began a few weeks after Christmas, my sister Molly started college.

The
Fireside
Book of
Ghost
Stories

THE PACKAGE WAS WRAPPED in red and white foil with a pair of candy canes stuck on like crossed swords. I'd saved it for near the end because I expected something special, but when the wrapping fell away I felt a stab of disappointment. Uncle Jonathan had finally slipped.

Did you ever notice how each year your favorite present seems to come from the same person? In my case it's my Uncle Jonathan. I hardly ever see him, but at Christmas and on my birthday each year his presents arrive. All my life he has seemed to know what I wanted before I knew myself. The toy Dalmatian he sent when I was four was the stuffed toy I dragged around all day and took to bed with me at night. Then the year my mother said "no guns," Uncle Jonathan sent me a space gun. He gave me a set of knights in armor and a toy sword. He had even sent some good books: *Captain Blood*, *Kim*, *Tom Sawyer*. But the book inside the package with the candy canes was a thick, old, tan volume that looked as though it had been dropped in a mud puddle.

The lower half of the book was swollen from having been wet. The cover was mildewed, and the pages had water stains running halfway up. The spine was torn. It didn't look like the kind of thing I'd have given to anybody, especially a favorite nephew at Christmas. Maybe he'd decided I wasn't worth it anymore. Or maybe he'd gotten out of touch with people my age.

I was into electronics that year. Everything I had asked for was high-tech, new, shiny, and complicated. A book of stories—an old, beat-up book—was the last thing I wanted.

I put the book aside without even reading its title, which was practically worn off anyway.

Later that afternoon Uncle Jonathan called to wish us Merry Christmas. When it was my turn to speak to him, he said, "Nathan! What did you think of the book?" Then without giving me a chance to answer, he went on, "I got it when I was twelve, so I figured you'd be about the right age. That was always one of my favorites. Treat it well."

I mumbled and stumbled over thanking him. Treat it well? It didn't look as though he'd treated it very well himself. As soon as I was off the phone, I headed back to the tree, searched among the paper and pulled out the book. I might not want it, but it had been embarrassing not even to know the title of the book he'd sent. And he'd said it was one of his favorites, so he meant well.

As I opened it, a sheet of paper fell out. I retrieved the fallen paper with one hand while I read the title: *The Fireside Book of Ghost Stories.* Ghost stories?

I unfolded the sheet of paper that had fallen from the book and found that it was a letter from my uncle.

Dear Nathan,

I was about your age when I got this book. (Incidentally it wasn't new then. You'll notice it was published in the 1940s.) I hadn't believed in ghosts for several years by that time. This book changed my mind. You see, it isn't just about hauntings; it is haunted.

I know how that sounds, but you'll see what I mean. Or, maybe you won't. Either way you'll have good, classic ghost stories to read.

I say the book is haunted because of a story that used to be there and then suddenly wasn't there any longer. In addition, it seemed to me that I couldn't choose what I would read from this book. I've only been able to read what the book would let me find.

At six hundred pages, it's too long to read at one sitting, even if you could take that much horror at once. Also, there are more than forty stories listed in the table of contents. I know people would say that with so many stories, it was perfectly natural that sometimes a kid wouldn't be able to find a particular one. Let them say what they will; I know what I know.

Don't take my word for it. Read it for yourself.

Best,

Uncle Jon

After that letter, nothing could have kept me from reading a little of *The Fireside Book of Ghost Stories* that very afternoon. I can't say I noticed anything strange about the book, apart from its graveyard smell of mildew, but the two stories I read were spine-chillers.

The first one was called "The Room in the Tower," a scary story where the horror kept building each time you read the words "Jack will show you to your room. I have given you the room in the tower." The words are from a nightmare, and the reader knows that someday the narrator is going to hear them in reality. That was a good story.

The only other one I read on Christmas Day was called "Murder Will Out," a really old story from *The Canterbury Tales*. I just read it because it was short, not expecting to like it much. But things like "thou art" and "revealest" didn't bother me. That one was pretty good too.

Uncle Jonathan was right about one thing. Nobody would read forty or so stories like that all at once. So I put the book on my shelf and over the months picked it up and read a story once in a while. I wouldn't have admitted it at the time but I never read that book in bed at night. I read the ghost stories on Saturdays or when I got home in the afternoons. They just weren't the kind of thing you want to have in mind when you're trying to fall asleep in the dark.

I guess it would be true to say I came to like that book. It hadn't made much of a first impression with its stained pages and moldy smell, but I was still reading the book when I had forgotten about most of the other presents from that Christmas.

I also found that I would pick up the book intending to reread one story and would end up reading something entirely different. Unlike my uncle, I didn't think some sort of magic had substituted one story for another. Some of the stories' names weren't very memorable. I'd try out two or three possibilities and then, not finding the one I was looking for, settle in to read something else. It wasn't supernatural. I mean the book wasn't hiding the story I was looking for or forcing me to read another one.

For instance, one tale was about a room haunted by the spirit of a wicked old woman whose heirs had turned her mansion into a boardinghouse. At first, the heirs, who reminded me of the brother and sisters in *Arsenic and Old Lace*, were unaware of the evil in the house. Then they found that none of the boarders would stay in one particular room. The sister who did the cleaning began to get scared to go into the room.

Finally, the sister who did the cooking said she'd move into the room herself. I liked that story because things turned out fine for the sisters and their brother while what happened in between was as scary as anything I've ever read.

Somehow, I could never quite remember the name of that one, so I'd end up looking up anything that had "room" in the title. Naturally, I could never find it when I was deliberately looking for it because the word "room" isn't in the title at all. I figured I had discovered the secret of Uncle Jonathan's "haunted book." Stories didn't disappear; they were hard to find because of their forgettable titles.

I read that book off and on for more than a year. Then midway through my thirteenth year, I put it away and forgot it.

When Uncle Jonathan came to visit us soon after I turned fifteen, I remembered the book again. I asked him what his "disappearing" story had been about.

He glanced at me sharply. Then he grinned and shook his head.

"I'll tell you about it someday. Not now."

That was all I could get out of him. But once again I got out *The Fireside Book of Ghost Stories* and began to read it.

My best friend is Tom McHenry, who's on the swim team with me. That summer we were finally old enough to qualify as counselors at a local camp. I know ghost stories are popular at camp, so I packed up Uncle Jonathan's book to take along with me.

Sure enough we fell into the habit of telling ghost stories, mostly silly but scary ones with lots of dramatic effects, to the kids around the campfire. The stories we were telling were nothing like the ones in my book, but they prompted me and Tom to discuss ghost stories in general. We discovered we'd both read quite a few. I offered to let Tom read some of *The Fireside Book of Ghost Stories*.

"Have you ever read this one, the one called 'Friends'?" he asked one day.

I didn't remember the title, so I took the book to
read the beginning of the story. I didn't recognize it,
but it caught my interest, and I read the whole thing
through.

The story was about two friends called Nicholas and
Arthur, who lived in Victorian England. The story took
place around Christmastime. Although there was ice
covering the river behind Arthur's house, the boys had
been forbidden to skate on it because it was too thin
in spots.

Not long before Christmas, the two went out with
a wooden sled to cut holly. When the sled was loaded,
they put on their skates (which they just happened to
have brought with them) and began to skate home
along the frozen river, pulling the sled.

About halfway home, they skated over a thin
patch of ice that broke when the heavy sled was
pulled over it. The sled went through the ice, pulling
Nicholas down with it. But Arthur managed to escape.
He scrambled out onto the nearest bank and looked
around for an old fence rail, the limb of a tree,
anything he could safely extend to his friend.

While he searched, Nicholas disappeared beneath
the water. Certain that he no longer had a hope of
saving his friend, Arthur removed his skates and hid
them. He then went home and told his father about
the accident, claiming that Nicholas had insisted on
pulling the sled along the river but that he, Arthur, had
refused to go out onto the ice and had followed along
on the bank. The grief-stricken families, his own and

Nicholas's, believed his story and praised him for doing the right thing.

Then, on Christmas morning, Arthur was found dead in his bed, his body encased in ice.

"Not the sort of story we can tell our campers," Tom said, laughing, when he saw I had finished reading. "The kids would rather have escaped lunatics and hatchet murders."

It seemed odd that I had never seen the story before, but I figured there must be half a dozen or more stories in the book that I had never read. Still, the gruesome tale drew me, and I read it several times over the next few weeks.

I read it too often. That story got into my dreams. Like a refrain, the same words would show up in dream after dream: "It wasn't my fault. It's too late to save him."

Like those nightmare words about Jack showing the way to the tower, those sentences were enough to start me trembling. In my dreams, instead of Arthur and Nicholas, Tom and I were the main characters. I could see dark, swirling waters and Tom would slip out of sight each time I tried to reach him.

I'd wake up scared to death and have to lie there telling myself that Tom is as good a swimmer as I am.

By daylight I'd think the dreams were stupid, but at night I'd break into a sweat of fear.

One night while I was once again dreaming of trying to rescue Tom from murky water, I seemed to feel my sweat turning to specks of ice all over me. I woke up terrified.

I looked carefully around the cabin where ten boys were also sleeping, counted them to make sure everyone was safe, and then checked Tom's bunk. He was there, sleeping peacefully.

The following day I wrote to Uncle Jonathan and asked him again if he'd tell me the story of his own strange experience with *The Fireside Book of Ghost Stories*. It seemed to me that the story "Friends" was haunting my dreams, and I hoped my uncle would say something that would help. I addressed and stamped the letter and dropped it into the mailbox where the campers posted their letters to parents. But, as soon as the letter was through the slot, I was sorry I'd sent it. Uncle Jonathan would think I was some sort of idiot not to have known he was joking. I shrugged and hoped he wouldn't take my letter seriously.

Night after night the dreams continued and I continued to wake up and check the people in my cabin. About a week later I woke up in the middle of an especially hot night. Out of habit, I checked the cabin. The first thing I saw was that Tom was gone, probably outside cooling off. As usual, I checked each bed and saw the boys sleeping—more restlessly than peacefully but at least sleeping. And then I saw that one camper's bunk was also empty.

I slipped soundlessly out of bed and out of the cabin. In the moonlight, I saw no one but thought I heard noises from down the hillside.

I plowed straight down the cliff for a few yards.

Then I cut through a narrow crevice, clambered over tumbled rocks at the foot of the hill, and looked out over a natural pool with a foot-bruising rocky edge. This pond was off-limits for campers, who had the use of a chlorinated, olympic-sized pool at the campsite, as well as a lake higher up in the hills.

"Tom!" I called as I saw him pulling himself up onto the rocks from the water.

"Let's go," he said as soon as he was out of the water. "We have to get back before anyone misses us. Just forget we ever came out."

"What are you talking about? What happened? Do you know that one of the campers is missing? That kid Mitchell is not in the cabin."

"I know. He's in there." Tom gestured with a dripping hand toward the pool. "I trailed him down here and saw him dive in. He must have hit his head. It's pretty shallow and there're rocks everywhere. Anyway, he didn't come up. I've dived and dived, but I can't find him. It wasn't my fault. It's too late to save him."

His words knocked the wind out of me like a fist into my solar plexus. The nightmare feeling closed around me.

I seemed to be about three feet above the scene, watching with frozen disinterest. Tom was still talking. But I couldn't hear him. I wasn't thinking. I just acted. My body arced into the air, and I didn't give a thought to the rocks just below the surface. In a shallow dive I cut into the water that was as cold as a river in winter.

When I plunged under the surface, body and awareness merged. Just as I'd done over and over in my dreams, I went searching beneath black waters. I stayed under, feeling among the rocks in a world where sight was useless, until I thought my lungs would burst.

I would have to go up for air.

As I was ready to push for the surface, my foot touched something that was not rock. I'd found Mitchell.

I grabbed, pulled, lifted, took a secure hold, and struck out for the rocky shoreline.

At the water's edge, Tom met me and between us we lifted Mitchell over the rocks to a leaf-covered patch of ground where we fell to work reviving him. Long seconds passed and stretched into minutes. Tom, ashamed at having quit too soon, pushed me aside and took over. Driven by nightmare-horror on my part and shame on his, neither was going to quit too soon this time. On and on we tried. And then, Mitchell coughed and at last began to breathe.

Two days later I got a three-page letter from Uncle Jonathan, who hadn't laughed at my request. When he was sixteen, he wrote, he had read and reread a story in *The Fireside Book of Ghost Stories* about a boy whose meetings with a ghost prepare him for his father's death.

After summarizing the story, Uncle Jonathan said:

I seemed to slip into that story and live it. And the story got into my dreams. I felt that I knew the characters. When the boy in the story finally learned to accept pain and death and go on living, I learned it too. I had read stories before that meant something to me. I'd even picked up a lesson or two from things I'd read, but this was the first time a story had so much impact that it changed me.

I remembered the name of the story as "Destiny," but in later years when I went back to find it there was no story of that title listed. I figured I'd gotten the name wrong, so I eventually read through the whole book looking for the story. I never found it again. But that search was much later, long after my sixteenth year, after I no longer needed the story.

The months when I read and reread the story were the months just before my mother died. I think I accepted my own grief with more maturity because through that haunted book I had already known what it was like to lose a parent.

I folded the letter, put it back into its envelope, and went to find *The Fireside Book of Ghost Stories.* No such story as "Destiny" was listed. For curiosity sake, I went back to the beginning of the list of forty-one titles and looked for "Friends."

I went through it once and then again. No story in the book was called "Friends." One story was called "Playmates," but it was about a little girl who had ghostly playmates to keep her company. Arthur and Nicholas and the sled loaded with holly weren't any part of it.

I tried all the more likely titles without finding it. Then I asked Tom about the story since he'd been the one to read it first. But he shrugged and said he didn't remember.

I'm still searching. It has to be there—*The Fireside Book of Ghost Stories* was the only book I had at camp.

A
Ride
on the
Dumbwaiter

THE CAR TURNED beside a low brick wall and wound up a steep, curving drive. When they came to a stop, Sam saw the house for the first time. Made of stone and wood, it had everything—a tower, an outside staircase, a porch that ran around three sides of the house, a little balcony on the second floor. The house was three stories tall, and probably had a basement and an attic besides.

Aunt Liz led the way up to the front door with Sam and his cousin Jeremy following.

"Keep an eye on your cousin," Aunt Liz told Sam, who at age twelve was the older of the two, "and try to stay out of my way."

Sam knew what it was like to be stuck with a younger kid, and Jeremy was the worst! That kid got into everything.

Sam led his young cousin down the front hall toward the back of the house. They might as well have

a good look at the old mansion. Aunt Liz was part of a
group that planned to turn the house into a museum.
Built more than two centuries earlier, it was filled with
antiques and had a long history. Aunt Liz said that at
one point the house had belonged to a man who'd
made his fortune in railroads. The only other thing Sam
remembered his aunt saying was that one of the owners
of the house had been a crazy old woman who had a
reputation for murder. Sam wasn't sure if that was true
or just a rumor.

At the end of the hall, Sam and Jeremy pushed open
a swinging door and found the kitchen. Cabinets ran
right up to the top of the ceiling, which looked about
a mile above Sam's head.

Seven-year-old Jeremy began opening cabinets.
"They're almost empty," he told Sam and crawled
inside one.

"Come on out of there," Sam called through the
door that had swallowed Jeremy.

"It's all open back there, like a tunnel. You can
crawl from one end of the kitchen to the other, and
it's empty," Jeremy said, climbing out a door at the far
end of the cabinet.

"Not quite empty," Sam told him, brushing a
clump of cobwebs out of Jeremy's hair.

Jeremy broke free from his cousin and began
tugging at a knob halfway up the wall.

"It's an elevator," he announced as the door
flew open.

"No, it isn't. It's too small."

"It's an elevator for food."

"You mean a dumbwaiter!" Sam exclaimed, pushing past his young cousin to see for himself. "It's so big. You could put a whole roast pig in here."

"I'm going in," Jeremy said, climbing in as he spoke.

Spending a day helping his aunt keep an eye on Jeremy had never been Sam's idea of fun. Jeremy was the kind of kid who would jump through a window without looking to see how far away the ground was.

"The rope that holds the dumbwaiter is old. It could break!" he told his young cousin.

"I think if I just push this button, it will go up," Jeremy said, ignoring Sam.

"Jeremy, get back here!'

"I'm going up."

At the last possible moment, Sam tumbled through the door of the dumbwaiter, and the two boys began to rise through the walls of the old house.

When they came to a stop, Jeremy grabbed the door and pushed.

"I can't get the door open."

Sam tried, but it wouldn't budge for him either.

Then he put his feet against the door and pushed with his back against the opposite wall. To the boys' amazement, the wall at Sam's back opened. After a moment's confusion, they turned around and crawled out the opposite side from the one they had entered.

They found themselves in what looked like a closet with shelves of dishes on both sides of them. As they stood hesitating, the door in front of them was flung open.

"What a racket you're making! Don't you know she's in bed? Not that she's likely to be sleeping with all the noise you two made. Now come out here where I can see you," said a woman in a nurse's uniform.

A thin screech sounded. The woman, who was blocking the very same door she had ordered them to come out of, said, "Now you've done it. You'll have to come in where she can look at you."

Sam walked out in front of Jeremy, using one arm to shield the younger boy. Following the brisk steps of their discoverer, the two children entered a bedroom dominated by a high, old-fashioned, four-poster bed. Sitting up on the bed and nearly hidden under a frilled cap was an old lady.

"Let me get a look at them," she commanded.

With Sam in the lead, the two approached her.

"Which of you is Archie?" she demanded.

"I'm Sam and this is my cousin Jeremy," Sam told her. "We came from the kitchen."

"The cook's boys, are you? Don't you have proper clothes? I thought you were that boy Archie. He comes from foreign parts, probably dresses funny too. I don't expect I'll like him either."

"I think we should be going. Honest, we didn't know there was anyone in the house. I'm sorry we disturbed you."

The two had just reached the door when Jeremy said, "She looks like a dragon."

At the door the nurse met them, asking, "Are you going?"

"Yes," Sam said, almost running. "We didn't mean to disturb her."

"Not that way," the nurse said, as Jeremy opened the door to the closet containing the dumbwaiter. "You'll have to take the stairs down."

She led them to a narrow flight of stairs that Sam guessed must lead back to the kitchen area. "Straight down and you'll be back in the servants' quarters." She turned abruptly and left the children.

"They were scary," Jeremy said, as the nurse walked back through the bedroom door. "Especially the woman in the bed."

"I know, but I don't know why. Who do you suppose they are? They seem to live here, but I thought your mother said the house was deserted."

"Pss-sst!" someone called.

"Who are you?" Jeremy asked, looking up to find a boy bending out over the stairs from the floor above them.

"Can you come up?" the boy called. "I didn't know there were any other children in the house."

"Neither did we," Sam answered. He and Jeremy scrambled up the stairs to face a tall, lean, blond boy about Sam's age.

"What are you doing here?" Jeremy asked.

"It's where we're going to live."

"I don't think so. It's going to be a museum as soon as Aunt Liz's committee can get it fixed up."

"I don't know anything about that. I believe the house belongs to my new father's family."

"I'm Sam and this is Jeremy," Sam told the other boy.

"I'm Archie Phipps," the boy replied. "I didn't expect to find anyone under eighty here. My mother and my new father have left on their wedding trip. The only person I've talked to so far is Mrs. Lowell, the woman who was trying to send you downstairs."

"Maybe you should come downstairs with us and meet Aunt Liz, that's Jeremy's mother. She doesn't know there's anyone living here."

As the three boys walked down the stairs, Jeremy explained to Archie about riding the dumbwaiter. "This is a great house," he said. "I wish I could live here, too. But I wouldn't like to live with that mean old woman. I don't think she wanted us here."

"Maybe you can come to visit. I don't know anybody yet."

"Come on in here," Sam said, pushing open the swinging door to the kitchen. He stepped back and dropped his hand so swiftly that the door bounced, almost slamming into his nose.

"What's wrong?" Archie asked.

"There are people in there."

"But you'd expect to find people in the kitchen, wouldn't you?" Archie asked. "I've heard there are cooks and servants and all kinds of people here."

A prickling started behind Sam's eyes and a tingle ran over his scalp.

"I don't know what's going on," he said. "But when Jeremy and I left that kitchen twenty minutes ago, it was bare and ugly and almost everything in it was painted green. Now there are three women in aprons in it and every cabinet is painted white with red trim."

"It couldn't have been empty. Somebody has to cook for Mrs. Rosemont."

"Who is Mrs. Rosemont?"

"My new grandmother, the lady Mrs. Lowell is nurse to."

Through teeth that were almost chattering, Sam said, "Come on, Jeremy. Let's go find your mother."

He grabbed his young cousin and hurried toward the sitting room with Archie following them.

The front hall was cleaner and brighter than it had been earlier, different also in some way Sam didn't pause to define. Reaching the sitting room, he found it spotless in the sunshine. Aunt Liz was nowhere in sight.

"There you are," a voice boomed. All three children turned to face the nurse. "Mrs. Rosemont is resting, but she will see you, Archie, when she wakes. I must insist on absolute quiet until that time."

Jeremy picked that moment to panic. "Where's my mother?" he bellowed.

"Get out of here!" the nurse roared.

"I'll just see them out," Archie said, catching an elbow of each of the others and steering them toward the rear of the house.

As soon as they were out of earshot of the nurse, Sam said, "We have to talk."

The trio slipped through an open door, and Archie closed it behind them. For a moment they just looked at each other.

"We came to a vacant house because my aunt, who is Jeremy's mother, is on a committee that will open the house as a museum," Sam explained. "We came to an old, vacant house, filled with dusty furniture but no people. We took a ride on a dumbwaiter and found ourselves in a clean house filled with people."

"I arrived here last night to stay with Mrs. Rosemont while Mother and my stepfather go on their wedding trip. I've seen half a dozen servants since I came, but I've spoken to no one except Mrs. Lowell and you two."

"This is the same house we were in this morning when we arrived, but it's different. I know we're still in the same place. Are you sure this isn't a joke?"

"I'm not part of a joke. My name is Archibald McGregor Phipps, and I was born June 14, 1922. I was twelve my last birthday."

Sam felt like he was freezing. His teeth began to chatter.

"You'd be twelve in 1934! I don't believe it."

"I've told you the truth."

"Oh, I believe you. I just don't believe this is happening. You see, for us, 1934 was a long time ago, before my grandfather was born!"

Jeremy began to cry.

"We'll get back," Sam promised, putting his arm around his cousin.

"It isn't really so bad, old man," Archie said. "It's just a bit of an adventure, you know. A couple of twists and turns through this big old house and we'll have you right back where you were. And I've met two chums in the meantime. You wouldn't begrudge me that, now would you? I was all on my own until you two showed up."

Sam looked at Archie with appreciation. It wasn't the sort of talk he had ever heard from the twelve-year-olds he knew, but it was just what was needed to get Jeremy back into good spirits.

"What do we do next?" Jeremy asked, snuffling away the last of his tears.

"That's the spirit! We'll take the front stairs this time. I think we can get back to my room without running into Mrs. Lowell again. We have some planning to do."

Creeping along, the three boys mounted the stairs, with Archie leading the way.

At the top of the steps on the third floor, Archie motioned for silence, listened a moment, then led the way to a door halfway down the hall. They all stayed silent until the door was closed behind them. Archie still kept a finger to his lips and pointed to the opening above the door. Gently, he closed the transom.

"I think it's safe enough now. Have a seat."

Two large trunks and several boxes covered the floor space. Sam and Jeremy each chose a seat.

"You said you were just here for a visit," Sam said. "It looks like you've moved in."

"My mother and her new husband are going to live here when they come back from their wedding trip, so it's my new home, too, at least until I go away to school."

"I don't think Mrs. Rosemont is going to like having you here. She doesn't seem to like kids."

"Maybe she's ill."

"*I* think she's crazy."

Sam cast a sidelong glance at Jeremy, who seemed to have recovered from his fear, though Sam wasn't sure the younger boy realized they were stuck in the 1930s in the house of a strange, maybe crazy, old lady.

Archie seemed to read Sam's thoughts.

"I wonder," he said to Jeremy, "if you'd be interested in my collection of arrowheads."

"Would I? Neat!"

Archie opened the trunk he had been using as a seat, lifted out the upper tray, and picked up a box wrapped in a woolen scarf. Carefully unwinding the scarf, he handed the box over to Jeremy.

"You can lay them out on the bed. I have all kinds, some for arrows, some for spears." Archie pointed out a white quartz arrowhead as his personal favorite. A few moments later, he left Jeremy to the wonders of the collection and returned to sit on the floor beside Sam.

"This isn't the house we came into this morning," Sam began. "At least, it may be the same house, but this certainly isn't the same time period."

"While I don't fancy losing the only friends I've found here," Archie answered softly, "I can quite see that you'll have to go back. The question is how."

They suggested possibilities and discarded them, until their talk drifted away from solving the problem of time travel and centered instead on their own interests and lives. Sam talked about his soccer team at school and about favorite movies. Archie told about his horse named Lady Velvet that had been left behind in St. Louis and about his journey by train, with cars for sleeping and cars for dining, across the country to this new home where he'd felt pretty uncomfortable until Sam and Jeremy showed up.

They forgot their present problem until Jeremy said, "I think we'd better be going. It's been fun, but my mom may be looking for us by now. Come on, Sam. We have to find the stupid elevator."

"Dumbwaiter," Sam corrected automatically.

"It can't hurt to try," Archie said, standing up. "The dumbwaiter brought you here. It just may take you back."

"Except that the dumbwaiter is in a pantry outside Mrs. Rosemont's room. How are we supposed to sneak past Mrs. Lowell?"

"Come on, you two. We can at least give it a try."

They crept from the room, down the hall, down one flight of stairs, and into the pantry. Footsteps sounded on the wooden floor just as Archie closed the pantry door behind the three of them.

"Just remember," he cautioned the others, "if this doesn't take you back to where you came from, come and find me. Promise?"

A rattle at the door warned them that Mrs. Lowell had found them. Archie closed the door to the dumbwaiter and set it in motion.

"So there you are! What on earth are you doing in the pantry?" Sam and Jeremy heard Mrs. Lowell saying, as they slid slowly down through darkness.

Sam remembered to watch for the door on the opposite wall from the one they had entered. A sliver of light appeared beneath them. *The door into the kitchen*, Sam thought. Then the dumbwaiter stopped, close enough for the two boys to see the opening below them but too far away for them to reach it.

"No!" Sam exclaimed.

"Are we stuck?" Jeremy asked.

Before Sam could answer, motion resumed with a faint whirring.

"We're going back up," Jeremy said.

He was right; the dumbwaiter was now carrying them upward, back to the second-floor pantry.

As it came to a stop, the door was opened for them.

"I thought I heard the dumbwaiter, and I suspected I'd find you here. Didn't I ask you to leave?"

"Just let us ride the dumbwaiter. We'll leave," Jeremy offered.

"Out! Both of you, out of there."

Unwillingly, the two cousins emerged to face an irate Mrs. Lowell. She caught Jeremy by his ear in a hold that left him shouting "Ouch!" while his eyes streamed. With a firm grasp of Sam's shoulder, she led the pair out of the pantry.

"What is this?" called the shrill voice the children now knew for Mrs. Rosemont's.

"I hope they haven't disturbed you. I'm just going to see them out."

"Let them come in here a moment."

"Yes, Mrs. Rosemont. Perhaps you'd like Archie to see them out."

"Archie is gone. He won't be coming back."

Mrs. Lowell shook her head and looked puzzled, but she left the children just inside the door of Mrs. Rosemont's bedroom and closed the door softly behind her.

Muttering "beastly little demons," Mrs. Rosemont turned away from them to pace in front of the fireplace, rubbing her hands and mouthing words they couldn't understand.

Sam looked around the room and saw that it was crowded with big, old pieces of furniture.

"Let's get out of here," Jeremy wailed, tugging at Sam.

"Wait," Sam begged. "Jeremy, I think Archie is still here."

"Where?"

"I don't know. I just don't think he would have gone away without first being sure we were gone."

"Do you think Mrs. Rosemont did something with him?"

"She may have. I want to look around."

Sam swiftly reached out and turned the knob on the mirrored door of the clothes press beside him.

Catching the spirit of the search, Jeremy dropped to his knees and peered under the high bed.

"I hear something knocking," Jeremy shouted, attracting the attention of Mrs. Rosemont.

"You dreadful, eavesdropping creature!" she cried from beside the fireplace.

"Look! The chest is rocking!" Jeremy cried.

"Spy!" Mrs. Rosemont shrieked at him. "Watching, listening, prying! I'll get rid of the lot of you." She turned toward the fireplace and tugged a poker free from the rack of implements.

"Quick!" Sam urged, pulling a fringed silk scarf off the chest from which they could hear bumps.

"There's a key in the lock," Jeremy said, as he bent down to look.

"Look out!" Sam cried, dragging Jeremy to the floor with him at the same moment the poker crashed across the top of the chest.

Mrs. Rosemont raised the poker and took aim for a second blow.

Sam pushed Jeremy out of the way, grabbed the edge of the rug on which Mrs. Rosemont stood, and jerked it.

"Stop!" shouted a male voice, as the old woman fell to the floor.

A strange man bent down to help Mrs. Rosemont up. Mrs. Lowell appeared in the open door, mouth agape.

"It's all right," the man said soothingly to Mrs. Rosemont, as he slipped the poker out of her grip.

Sam pulled himself to a sitting position. Jeremy raised his head from the floor and looked around in wonder.

"She was going to kill us," the younger boy exclaimed in wonder.

"Nonsense, she was only—" Mrs. Lowell began but was quelled by a look from the man.

"Careful, now. I think you should lie down and rest, Mother."

Mother? Was this man Archie's new stepfather? Sam wondered. He made a fresh grab for the key in the lock of the chest. His hand closed over the key, and this time he opened it without interference.

"Archie!" Jeremy cried, as the lid of the chest was lifted.

Sam caught Archie's hand to help him climb out of the chest.

"Great Scott!" the man exclaimed. "Is he all right? That trunk is airtight."

"I thought he had gone. I believed she had frightened him away," Mrs. Lowell said, twisting her hands in her apron.

"Take care of my mother," the man said sternly. "She should rest now."

"I knew you'd come back," Archie was saying as he gasped for breath and beamed at Sam and Jeremy. "As soon as she trapped me, I concentrated on wishing you back again."

"Are you all right?" the man asked again.

"Yes, sir. I believe so."

"Bring him outside for a breath of air."

Sam, Jeremy, and Archie followed the man out of
the room, down the hall, and out through a door that
led to the upstairs balcony. Even with his attention
focused on Archie, Sam noticed that the whole hill on
which the house stood was thick with trees. If there
were other houses nearby, they were hidden from view
by tree trunks and the curve of the hill. He shook his
head and sighed, wondering if they would ever get
back to the present and Aunt Liz and the cheeseburgers
she had promised them for lunch.

The man misinterpreted Sam's sigh. "My mother
isn't well," he said. "She isn't accountable. Mrs. Lowell
should never have left her alone with a child."

"Is this your new father?" Jeremy asked.

"I'm Lionel Rosemont, Archie's new uncle, though
we haven't met before," he said, holding out a hand,
which Archie promptly took. "We both seem to be
indebted to the two of you."

"I'm Sam and this is my cousin Jeremy."

"Well, Sam and Jeremy," Mr. Rosemont said, smiling
for the first time and suddenly looking much nicer.
"We're both grateful to you. Perhaps I can see about
lunch for all of us. Archie, would the three of you like
to wait here? I assure you there is nothing more to fear.
I want to have a word with Mrs. Lowell, and then we'll
have lunch."

"I'm afraid we can't—" Sam began. On second
thought, he said, "It's very kind of you to ask us
to stay."

How could he tell Mr. Rosemont they couldn't stay when the real problem was that they couldn't go?

"I'm sorry, Archie," Jeremy said, as soon as the door had closed behind Mr. Rosemont. "I think this is why we couldn't get away when we tried." Jeremy pulled from his pocket an arrowhead, a white quartz one marked with a streak of dark orange lightning. "I shouldn't have taken it."

Archie laughed. "You can have it. I'm grateful for whatever brought you back."

Jeremy shook his head. "No, thanks. I want to go home now."

"Why did she shut you in that trunk?" Sam asked.

"I don't know," Archie said, pocketing the arrowhead Jeremy insisted on giving him. "As soon as I stepped into the room, I saw her holding up the lid of the trunk and looking in. She said, 'Here, boy, see if you can get my brooch for me.' So I walked over and looked into the trunk. It looked empty, but she pointed and said, 'There, in the corner. Reach in and get it for me.' So I leaned over, and she pushed me in and shut the lid."

"Just like the witch who pushed Hansel and Gretel into the oven," Jeremy said.

"Let's see what we can do about getting you out of here," Archie said. "Follow me."

Sam and Jeremy followed Archie to the third floor, where he led them to a small square door about three feet above the floor.

"I think the dumbwaiter can deliver things to this

floor, too."

He opened the door and all three poked their heads into the shaft of the dumbwaiter.

"There are some buttons here," Jeremy said, pressing one as he spoke.

With its familiar whir, the box on the floor below them began to move upward, at first smoothly, then haltingly. With a jolt, it came to a stop halfway between the floors.

Sam's heart seemed to stop with it, but Archie was still staring at the dumbwaiter.

"I think I see the problem," he said. "There's a bit of a twist in the cable. If I can just straighten that out, I think the dumbwaiter will come on up."

Before Sam could protest, Archie had swung both legs over the opening and was sitting on the edge of the wall below the door.

"I don't think you should climb down there," Sam told him.

"It's the only way."

"Then I should be the one to go. This is our problem."

Archie didn't bother to answer. He fell forward with his hands out, caught the cable, and began to work his way down.

"Are you okay?"

"Fine," he called, reaching the top of the dumbwaiter. He knelt and began to work at the twist that was blocking the elevator's progress. "Look, you two, if I get this kink out, the box will begin to move up again. Step back from the door, so I can jump through as it passes."

In one motion Sam and Jeremy stepped back.

"What if he can't jump off in time?" Jeremy asked.

The whir of the machinery starting up was his only answer.

Sam clenched both hands into fists.

And then Archie was there, framed in the doorway. Almost at once he tumbled through onto the floor beside them.

"Way to go!" Jeremy cried.

The dumbwaiter slid to a halt in front of the open door.

"You'd better go. My uncle will be coming for us soon."

"Will you be all right?" Sam asked.

"Will you?" Archie responded. "I'm much better off than if I hadn't met you."

"Tell your uncle we had to go."

"Wait!" Archie cried. "When you're gone, I'm going to feel that this never happened."

Sam fished a pencil out of his pocket. "Do you have a piece of paper?"

From his own trouser pocket, Archie brought out the stub of a train ticket. "Will this do?"

Sam took it and hurriedly scribbled on the back. "There," he said. "Keep this and you'll always know we were real."

Together, he and Jeremy scrambled into the dumbwaiter.

"Good-bye," Jeremy called before turning around in preparation for his exit at the end of the ride.

"Good luck," Archie replied. "I'll start you down."

Reluctantly, Archie gave one last wave and shut them into the darkness. At the same moment, the dumbwaiter began its descent.

"Are we heroes?" Jeremy asked in the twilight of the dumbwaiter passage.

"Heroes?"

"Yeah, for saving Archie's life."

"Mr. Rosemont probably would have saved him anyway." *And who knows if he is saved for good,* Sam thought. Mrs. Rosemont might try again—and succeed.

"I think we're heroes. Mr. Rosemont wouldn't have found him in time," Jeremy said.

"I hope we're home, heroes or not."

"It's okay. This time I left the arrowhead."

The dumbwaiter stopped with a light bounce. Sam braced himself to push the door open. Silently, he hoped they had made it all the way back to the kitchen—and all the way back to the present.

The door opened onto a cavernous, deserted, and sickly green kitchen. It looked great to Sam and Jeremy.

"Let's go find your mom."

"Wait'll we tell her!"

"Jeremy!" Sam said sharply. "I don't think—"

Jeremy didn't stop to hear. He was running down the hall.

Close on his heels, Sam catapulted into the sitting room where doors and windows were now thrown open on its dust and gloom.

"We're hungry," Jeremy said.

"I'm ready to break for lunch myself," his mother said.

"Was someone here?" Sam asked. Through an open window, with its heavy drapes propped back to let in air, he could see the sun flashing from a car as it turned out of the curving driveway back onto the street lined with houses.

"You two just missed the nicest man, but he said he couldn't stay to meet you. He was passing by and stopped in because he used to spend summers here when he was a boy."

"Maybe he knew Archie," Jeremy suggested.

His mother brushed the dust from her skirt and moved toward the fireplace. Sam shivered as he caught sight of a poker on the hearth.

"He said it was a great house for adventures. When I told him you two were exploring it today, he insisted on hearing all about you. He asked me to give you this, Jeremy."

From the mantle, Aunt Liz picked up a small object and dropped it into Jeremy's hand.

Sam moved over closer to see what Jeremy had been given, imagining a quarter or silver dollar.

Lying on Jeremy's open palm was a white arrowhead. He turned it over, and a streak of rust-colored lightning showed through the white quartz.

"Sam, he asked me to give this to the 'older of the two gentlemen.' "

Aunt Liz handed him a folded scrap of cardboard.

Sam opened it and saw it was the stub of an old railway ticket. He turned it over and read in his own handwriting, "Sam and Jeremy," and below their names today's date.

"Such a silly thing," Aunt Liz said, "but he was so serious about it. He said he couldn't possibly stay because it was 'an adventure for the young people.' "

"I wish he had stayed," Sam said. A laugh tickled deep in his throat. Halfway up it turned into a lump that made his eyes feel damp.

20349

J
F
VIV   Vivelo, Jackie

         Chills in the
         night

DUE DATE
